Ra

ISBN-13 978-1-60145-208-5
ISBN-10 1-60145-208-X

Printed in the United States of America.

Booklocker.com, Inc.
2007

Ragdoll Angel

A Novella

By

T.W. McNemar

For Kack

‘Through the eyes of a child, there is only truth.’

T.W.M. ‘97

INTRODUCTION

There was a Time . . .

For the first time in two decades, the people of America felt some degree of confidence. Working people wore crisp, sharp uniforms. They drove newer, more artfully designed cars. The houses were all similar and in neat little rows. Kitchens started to fill with helpful devices that plugged into electricity. The word 'modern' was used and with electric mixers and television, you felt as though you were part of the mystique.

The post-war era was the golden age of home delivery. On special days of the week or month, the finest products know to man were brought to the misses and displayed in their finest grandeur. Everything from canned goods, bread, milk, bread, and eggs came weekly. Household brushes, cleaning products, tools, and sweepers came on a monthly scale. Neighborhood merchants, sharpening specialists, and repairmen came, it seemed, when needed.

It was a time of order. Brazen criminals were put in their place. The gangs' of previous eras were quickly dealt with due to the modern technologies associated with crime fighting. With radio, politicians' speeches were heard the very moment the lies were uttered. With television and brilliantly colored cinema, we became an entertained public.

The scientific world witnessed the evolution of space-age plastics, large thinking machines called computers, vaccinations for killer diseases, and a television that showed color. It was an exciting time. The world was evolving.

But that was the real, mainstream world. West Virginia was just not the same. The region was and is peopled with a hardy lot. People whose ancestors' trails passed this way lifetimes ago and they saw the wonder and stayed to tame this harsh corner. A land that constantly heals the scars man calls civilization. People will come and people will go but the land will remember and dissolve and return.

And for one brief moment in time, in nineteen fifty-two. .

There was this place . . .

Oak Hill, West Virginia was a small village in the center of a plateau region of the Appalachian Mountains. This rolling plateau punctuated with towering hills reaching a quarter of a mile or better above the rest and equally disrupted with a steep charging river that had sawed itself a thousand feet below the massive shelf. Trains chugged nonstop carrying bounty reaped from beneath and above the Earth's shell. Hardwood timber, sprouting as easily as dandelions, filled flatcars and headed toward markets unknown. Fuel-coal and metallurgical coal seemed to tumble from the hillsides when the huge machines slashed through the crust of the planet. Derricks dotted the mountainsides and valleys where the oil-witches sensed promise from beneath.

1952 Oak Hill still had a hitching post at the courthouse and a blacksmith at the railroad crossing. On Sunday you could see cars dating from the turn of the century to the present and, on an occasion or two, a buggy and horse in front of one of the Oak Hill churches. Televisions were as rare as good reception and in some cases, electricity. Even if you owned a television, on Saturday night you would turn it off and listen to Hank and Minnie and Roy on the 'Opry' on the radio. The movie house was open on the weekends only and the lone usher wore his high school ball cap with the bill removed instead of the pillbox issued with the Paramount uniform. The newsreels preceding the feature showed Marilyn in Korea, DiMaggio swatting balls in New York, and Eisenhower campaigning in the farm belt. The band at the high school prom included a 'feller' to call the square dances. In the summer, the movie house competed with the 'Moonshine Drive-in Theater'. The high schoolers' preferring the drive-in was probably the reason behind an inordinate amount of fall weddings.

There were these folk . . .

People in Oak Hill wore hats. Be it as a fashion statement or as protection against the elements, the hats were a daily regimen. It was nothing to see a man walk into the courthouse wearing a felt Stetson, heavy linen work pants with suspenders, and a uniform shirt with his 'tall papers' hanging high out of a breast pocket. Heavy work boots covered his feet every day and were shined on Sunday.

Men wore bandanas around their necks. At first it was smart work apparel. A coal miner used his bandana to keep the dust from his mouth in a day before respirators. Trainmen used their bandanas for everything from wiping gauges to signaling. Timbermen kept saw dust out of their shirt collars. In a pinch, the bandana was used for first aid, lunch pail, and personal hygiene. After time, different colored bandanas became the trademark for different groups, the most formidable being the 'wildcat' striking coal miner and his red bandana. It is one origin of the moniker, 'redneck'.

The best part about belonging to the community of Oak Hill was just that. Everyone was accepted at face value. Oh, there were some who dreamed above the rest and those whose affiliations isolated them, but life in a small town has its law of returns, just as in larger arenas.

Prologue: Moving day

August 1, 1952. If you take Route 19 south and go about ten miles below Tenneytown, you can turn left onto a rock and mostly dirt road called Otter Run. As you travel down Otter Run through that valley, along that small stream, it'll lead you to a fork in the road. The left leg of that fork is marked with a steel pipe topped by a piece of sheet metal in the shape of an arrow imprinted with the number of a gas well and the name Cathedral Oil and Gas. That leg of the road seems to be more of a path, but that's the way you'll go, and you'll come up a grade to the elbow of that hill where it forms Otter Hollow.

The cool of the morning has wandered off to the shade of the woods and hills leaving the air hot and still. On this morning a woman and a child are staring down that road, waiting, and it's a quarter till ten. Staring down a hot dirt road won't keep a child occupied, not this child anyway. The birds are still sailing about finishing a breakfast of flyers and crawlers but the child bored of watching them and she consoled herself by quizzing her Mother.

"Who's gonna live here now, Mom?"

"Don't know, baby girl, I just don't know," said the Mother. She sat on the trunk while the child strolled heel to toe about with her wrists at delicate angles. It wasn't often the child got to wear her dress, but today was moving day.

"Who's gonna get our stuff, Mom?" said the child referring to the 'leavins'.

" Whoever wants 'em, darlin'."

"Well, I hope they take care of it."

"Me too, darlin', me too."

As the Mother shielded her eyes and tried focusing into the distance, the child dropped to a squat and smoothed a patch of loose dust and began sketching the house and herself in the cotton dress. Her Mother inhaled sharply at the sight of the child kneeling in the dirt.

The child jumped up and quickly wiped her hands on the dress. Realizing her error, the child whispered, "aw poop."

Her Mother brushed the dress off with enough force to remove the dust and to help her daughter remember to keep clean. At that moment the whine of a flathead six cylinder with the hydromatic drive of a '49 Dodge reached the hill's top as the old driver mercilessly ground second gear. When the new and improved auto shift transmission failed to engage the driver barked an expression that echoed past the girl and her mother unnoticed and within moments, the black sedan stood before them.

"You Hobert's girl?"

"Yes, yes I am. Are you Mister Freeland?"

"Was you expectin' somebody else? Put your gear in the trunk and get in. Best move if you 'spect to make that bus."

He gestured toward the child. "That yours?"

"Yes, she's my daughter…"

"Well get her in here. I ain't got all day."

The black sedan ground its gears, going into reverse and then again as it retreated from the hollow. A long steel antenna waved mercilessly with each turn of the car. Mounted on the driver's door was a 3000 candlepower spotlight.

"I worked with your daddy up at the Dutch Coal strip job before I was elected constable, you know. This ain't one of my constable duties. I'm doin' this on account o' I knowed your daddy. He was good people, he was. Now, where you goin' to agin?"

"Oak Hill," she said.

"Everybody's always goin' someplace. I say they're just runnin' to something or runnin' from something. That's just something I figured out from being in the law awhile. What you goin' to Oak Hill for, girl?" he said leaning close enough for her to smell the sour breath of the Prince Albert tobacco blended with the scent of an early morning aperitif of a budget lager beer.

"I got a job in Oak Hill."

"Oh. A job. Well, what is it with you, girl? Are you runnin' to something or runnin' away from something?" he asked with the wise knowing nod of a seasoned law man.

She smiled cordially and to his confusion replied, "Yep."

Lawrence Freeland focused on the road as the wooden match

lit the freshly rolled cigarette. He mumbled something unintelligible in reply as the smoke escaped his lungs with a cough and, with his best shift of the morning, the Dodge found high gear. The radio static cleared just enough to hear Hank Williams' "I'm So Lonesome I Could Cry" and much to the young mother's amazement and the child's amusement, the lawman turned up the volume and began singing along with the radio. With a steady whine from the transmission and a whine from the singing lawman, the car meandered its way on the twisting blacktop toward the bus stop at the Mountaintop Restaurant and Filling Station.

ONCE'T UP ON A TIME, (1952 to be exact)

As did many of the great coal barons before and since, T.G. Wells made a grand sum, moved to a grand hill, built a grand house, and garnered all he could to accentuate his grand noblesse. He delegated the management of his mines to his engineers and foremen to free him to follow new endeavors. He was sure they skimmed here and there, but the money continued to roll in.

With his normal duties in the capable hands of others, Wells bored with his mines. He decided to venture on, into other avenues of business opportunity, perhaps something new or modern, something that lent toward respectability, more respectability perhaps, than that of a mere coal digger.

His first new business venture came three years after World War II. Ol' Wells cornered enough stock in the Fayette County Bank to assume an active role in its day-to-day function. The bank had one teller's window and a desk at the other end of the narrow room. The board meeting had the semblance of a quilting bee. Wells moved on.

Over a period of the next few years, Wells tried his hand at truck and equipment sales, general construction, real estate, and even an explosives and mine supply company.

He once decided that he had conquered the lower earth as a miner, why not conquer the top of the earth as a farmer. One season.

He spent that growing season wondering weather or whether. He decided that if you weren't a philosopher going into farming, you sure as hell would become one. Good-bye farming.

The only thing that held his attention and interest was his television station. He had owned a television but whenever he wanted to watch it, it was a challenge to manipulate the antenna in an attempt to receive the distant Charleston station. Then, while on business in New York, and on a whim, Wells walked into Rockefeller Center and applied for an NBC franchise. The train ride back to Oak Hill included a stop at Washington to apply for a Broadcasting License. At the suggestion of a freethinking clerk, Wells applied for the station name "WELL".

Gradually the station became a reality. When the "WELL"

channel 4 was finally on the air, Wells waited for feedback from the public. None came. No one knew it was there. The few televisions in Oak Hill were still trying to watch the distant Charleston station.

Wells finally convinced the local merchants to do what the appliance stores in New York City had done. They simply left a television, tuned to Wells' station of course, playing in the display window. Business picked up.

Lastly, Wells hired a closet thespian who had come back from Broadway with his tail between his legs. This was a boon to both Wells and Darrell Carson. Darrell employed his energy as actor, director, and all jobs between. Darrell even penned the catch phrase 'You've come to W-E-L-L to bail out another evening of fun and entertainment.' Wells handled the finances and some sales in an attempt to break even.

Other than the television station and his mines, Wells had become content to remain at home. He held business meetings at the mine on Wednesday, the television station on Friday, and at home, in the kitchen, on Mondays.

All local challenges had been met. Wells had done all, seen all, or heard all that he felt he needed to. Now, at age sixty-one, he waited. Wells had spent so much time trying not to miss anything in life, that he missed one of its richest treasures, one that is never tiresome or boring. He had no family. He had married, twice in fact. One was a good and loyal wife, the other a gold digger. They both tired of being ignored and eventually parted. Wells, however, was not lonely . . . he couldn't see that far yet.

DOREEN

Doreen McIlhenney had been Wells' housekeeper since the house was completed. She was a large-boned pleasant-seeming lady, within a few years of Wells age. Occasionally, in earlier years, rumor had skirted the town regarding Wells and Doreen, rumor of no substance. Doreen always maintained her position as employee and always addressed her employer as 'Mr. Wells', and nothing else . . . to his face.

As the years passed, and Wells became more reclusive, Doreen's chores seemed to increase. He wandered about the big house, making messes here then there and more often of late, he would request dinner in his room.

Doreen would load the lacquered maple tray, trudge up the back twenty-one stairs, and walk the sixty-five paces to the den in Wells' bedroom. Wells would generally acknowledge the delivery of the meal with a grunt, then sit at the table and toy with the food while he stared down at the town and the valley beyond.

One day, in a very tired moment, Doreen approached her employer.

Wells glanced up across his reading glasses, "Well?"

"Well sir," she began, "I been pleasurably workin' for you for 'bout thirty six an' a half years or so now, an', well my hips and knee have been actin' up here more often than I deserve, an' well . . .uh. . .you're either gonna have ta' quit eatin' up in your room, or just fire me, or you could just hire me a helper, or something."

He knew this moment was coming and he dreaded losing Doreen. It had never occurred to him to just hire an assistant. "Who did you have in mind, Doreen?"

"Well, ah, ah...Mr. Wells, my, ah sister's second girl Helen is a real hard worker an' her husband hasn't been able ta' work since he come home from Korea an' her with a child that ain't no trouble at all an' she'd do 'bout anything that was asked . . . for the most part."

"Who, your niece or her daughter?"

Doreen hated Mr. Wells' ability to make light of other folk's way of putting words together. "Both of 'em, I guess." The smile was cordial, but the eyes were cold.

"Doreen, you could probably retire and get social security as well," said Wells.

Her eyes narrowed rapidly. "If that's how you'd treat me after all these years, well I'd not bring that girl in ta' this here house, an' besides, she don't know a thing 'bout how you like your food cooked an' clothes ironed nor nothin', ah . . . Mister Wells...sir!" Few dogs barked with less enthusiasm."

"And you said her husband was a cripple?" Wells asked as he absentmindedly sorted the mail.

"Well, no, not really. Nothin' really crippled 'bout him, 'cept his head. Some kinda shock from the war. That's why he lives down to the VA at Beckley, but she's real nice an' a real hard worker."

"Very well, bring her by for an interview, as soon as possible." An interview would be easier than continuing this conversation.

"Well thank ya ...Mister Wells... a lot."

As he watched her retreat to 'her kitchen', he could see the effort she put into her movement. He remembered the green-eyed spry lass she was in the beginning, but the bouncing brown hair had become a mix from the beauty parlor. The jaunty frame had been sculpted over, from her chin to her toes, with a layer of heavy clay it seemed. Doreen was a good girl, he would hire the niece regardless. She'd earned her helper and then some.

THE INQUISITION

The interview with Helen was the easiest Wells had ever done. The two ladies stood before Well's desk in his downstairs office, just down the long hall from the kitchen.

"Why Mister Wells, this here is my sister's girl, Helen," Doreen began, "an' Helen, this here is Mister Wells." All three smiled, on cue it seemed.

"Now Mister Wells, I know you'd be wantin' ta' ask this girl 'bout her last job an' her experience an' all, so I'll just save ya' the trouble an' tell ya' straight out. She ain't never worked before. Well, not for anybody but her-own-self an' her Mama 'course. But don't go ta' worryin' yourself none, cause she's cut from the same rug as me an' if you'd think I'm worth spit then she is too. But, far as payin' her, why I think a dollar an' ten cent is a fair start." Doreen's head spun from Wells to Helen to verify this stage of the negotiation. With their nod, she continued.

"Now, Helen will start with the upstairs work an' such, till I can teach her ta' handle the rest."

Now that Doreen was warmed up, she continued, "Now Helen, you'll be livin' up above the garage. There's a nice chauffeurs room up there an' since Mister Wells never had call for one, and why, it'd be a nice room for you'ns. It'll just need a little cleanin' is all."

With the interview behind them, Doreen dismissed all involved. "Why, if y'need us, we'll be down in the kitchen. I'll just be showin' her 'round an' all."

Wells leaned forward with a whimsical frown.

"What?" asked Doreen.

"That went quite well," Wells said. "I don't feel as if I left out anything."

"It don't feel like you did," Doreen agreed bluntly.

Helen and Wells exchanged a frown as the ladies walked down the hall. Wells glanced up again as the housekeepers retreated toward the kitchen. *'Helen is her name she said.'* Well Helen looked like no housekeeper he had ever seen. Her hands were worn and rough from hard work. Her posture was more athletic than just strong and she was tall enough and thin enough to be considered willowy. With the high cheekbones, slight overbite, and the shiny shock of reddish brown hair, she was quite striking. The old man glanced up again, “Goodness.”

Helen made a quick appraisal of her new employer as well. He stood a respectable height, wasn’t fat, dressed nice, and topped it with that wavy dark gray hair. He wore a tweed housecoat and with the sideburns, Helen thought he might be going for the plantation owner look. She quick-skipped a couple of times to catch up with Doreen.

A FAMILY McMURFREE

At seventeen, Helen had married her childhood sweetheart and gotten pregnant just in time for him to go off to save the world, as he knew it, from "them damn communists over there in Korea."

In a log bunker one hundred yards from the 38th parallel, Ted McMurfree had received a Red Cross telegram announcing Carol's birth. He had stared at the message without feeling. He couldn't imagine surviving this war, but he did.

Helen's sweetheart was returned. The package was intact, but the contents were pretty much destroyed. Ted could neither share nor release the grief and pain that lived inside him, so many patrols, so much death. So many times he walked back alone.

Helen tried to heal Ted the only way she knew how, by loving and mothering him. He cringed and cowered in response, drifting in and out of reality. Finally, he was admitted to the VA Hospital in Beckley for continuing psychological treatment. After many attempts at shock and drug therapy, Ted leveled out somewhat and was able to tolerate short visits. This was the main reason Helen wanted this job. It was much closer to Beckley. While she waited for Ted's improvement and for her next visit, she would occupy herself at Wells' mansion.

Wells had never gotten around to hiring a chauffeur, and as the years passed, the chauffeur's quarters had become filled with junk. Within two days time, Helen had organized, boxed and stored all of the room's contents. On the third day, she scrubbed the walls, polished the woodwork, and at midnight, she carried the sleeping little girl to her new bed, a trundle bed to the right of her own.

The apartment had a small bedroom, a full bath, and a living room and kitchenette combined. The stairway led down to a hallway that entered the garage, kitchen, or Doreen's room. This end of the house was Doreen's domain and everyone knew it.

Although tiny, the apartment was a palace compared to their old Yankee framed shack in Otter Holler. The old home had nothing to recommend it - a leaking tarpaper roof, water stained wall-rite, bare wooden floors, and broken windows patched with rags and tar. The only plumbing was a pitcher pump on the old galvanized sink, which served many purposes including weekly baths. Their bed was curtained off from the rest of the shack, and on the mantle above a coal burning grate leaned pictures of, Jesus, kneeling and prayin' by the light of a Gethsemane moon and a portrait of an awkward, frightened, shorn-headed country boy, in full dress uniform. The only other 'convenience' was exactly twenty-two steps out the back door and down a well-worn path.

When Doreen saw how fast and efficient Helen had organized her new living quarters, she laid plans to delegate work she hadn't felt like doing in years. Helen didn't mind the hard work. It kept her mind off her lonely bed – lonely since Ted had gone off to war, lonelier since he had returned.

Since their first conversation about hiring an assistant, no further mention was made to Wells about a child. He only ventured to the kitchen on Mondays at 7:00 a.m. and Carol was rarely awake at that hour. Even when she was awake, she was usually in Doreen's apartment watching the television. Helen had been at the Wells home more than a month, and the ladies had fallen into a nice routine. Helen cleaned the house and Doreen did the laundry, cooking, and shopping. Carol, so as not to be underfoot, remained in the apartment or in the kitchen with Doreen.

Carol and Doreen were instant buddies, cut from the same cloth, perhaps. Carol asked too many questions and missed nothing. If Doreen misplaced an item, like her car keys, Carol knew where to find it. If they were at the A & P or at Prince's Market and Doreen couldn't remember a certain item of the shopping list, Carol always did.

"Hey Aunt Doreen," yelled Carol over the noise of the washing machine one Monday morning, "How'sa come last time you used bluing and this time you used that smelly stuff in the brown jug. Although small, Carol had a voice in a range that few people could not hear, let alone ignore. Not quite shrill, not quite quiet, not quite soft . . . piercing perhaps, yeah, that's it.

"I was outa' bleach last time."

"Well, why didn't ya' just go to the store?"

"'Cause that's all I needed."
"So?!."

Carol always enjoyed the trips to the market. Here in Oak Hill, there was one adventure after another. With all that stuff on television and the trips to ol' Mr. Prince's store, the A&P Supermarket, or the G.C. Murphy's Five and Dime, Oak Hill was an amazing place to be, lots more amazing than that ol' holler where she had been born.

On Saturdays, Helen borrowed Doreen's Chevy and made the trip to Beckley to visit Ted at the VA. Ted's reaction to his therapy varied from week to week and Helen never knew what to expect when she entered his ward. Faithfully, she made the weekly trip in hope that he would calm enough to take Carol for another visit. The child hadn't been to the hospital for several months and Helen still believed the child would make a difference in his recovery. She patiently waited.

RELIGION...according to Doreen

Sundays were Doreen's day off. Before Carol's arrival, Doreen spent her Sundays in bed or at the Cloverleaf Inn, watching billiards or shuffleboard matches. These days, Doreen and Carol spent Sundays searching for a good church to join. Church, Doreen decided, was a good place to raise a kid.

They started out with the Presbyterian Church where Wells spent six Sundays each year. Doreen spotted a fellow housekeeper that she'd despised for years because of her gossipin' mouth and know-it-all attitude. Doreen and Carol moved on to the Methodist Church. Although Doreen had been raised as Methodist, she considered this congregation a little uppity. Carol thought they were just fine. Every Sunday, a new experience.

The next Sunday, they were off to yet another church. This time it was the Pentecostal Light of the Lord Church, over on Fox Grape Road. Carol liked the Sunday School and the singing. They used a guitar instead of a piano and she thought that was pretty neat.

The Pentecostal sermon, just like others, started slow, fervent, and solemn . . . kinda quiet-like. Then, the pastor's tongue sharpened and he began to peel those sins away like dry skin on a fat onion, layer after layer, just to get to the good.

Sitting next to Carol this day was an old bald man with new teeth. At the end of each of the pastor's breathless litanies, the old man yelled, "AMEN BROTHER!" and, as one might expect, his new teeth whistled just a bit. As the pastor neared the essence of his message, the old man with the whistling teeth, became so incensed that only whistling could be heard.

Doreen was annoyed. Carol was amused. The old man started to respond again and Carol noticed that the whistling slowed and stopped. As she watched, wide-eyed, he reached up, pulled out the new teeth, dropped them into the pocket of his jacket, and with increased fervor shouted, "AMEN!"

Well, poor little Carol cracked up. As the old toothless Christian turned toward her, she got a direct view of his bald head, gums, spittle, and spirit. She thought this was hilarious. As she giggled uncontrollably, she also tried to apologize to her aunt. "I'm sorry, I'm sorry!!" she hiccupped out between her bursts of laughter.

Doreen knew Carol well enough to understand. Were they not, after all, cut from the same piece of cloth? Unfortunately, no one else in the church understood. As she watched and giggled, the old man opened his mouth a bit wider and cocked his head to one side, like a confused dog. With that, the hapless child lost her last shred of control. Carol's high-pitched laughter mixed with the apology blended together into a cacophony of ecclesiastical madness.

It was at that precise moment that ol' Baldy knew in his heart that the child was speaking in tongues. He did the only thing he knew to do. He began to interpret.

He reached out with a shaking hand and grabbed Carol's arm and looking toward the heavens, began to incantate, "Thpeak through me and thith child, thweet Jethuth!!!"

Carol blew yet another cork. In the middle of her third attempt to apologize to her aunt, Doreen finally understood what Carol was trying to say. She was in dire need of a rest room. After a few tense moments, Doreen was able to wrestle Carol's arm away from the old timer in mid-translation and hurry Carol toward the ladies room.

Still shouting apologies mixed with high-pitched laughter, Carol's tears streamed down her cheeks like small rivers. As they passed through the church, everyone wanted to touch the blessed child. Many closed their eyes to ponder Carol's cries as they echoed through the old wooden church. Some repeated them. The pastor knew it was a prophecy. The church was filled with joy, awe, and elation. When she heard the pastor repeat and chant Carol's phrase, Doreen was filled with dread.

"GODAPEE, GODAPEE, GODAPEE!!!" Carol hailed as they passed down the aisle, out the door, and until they reached the outhouse beside the church.

On the way home, they remained silent, except for a few residual giggles from Carol. When Doreen laughed, she turned toward the window so Carol wouldn't see her. As they pulled into the driveway, Carol asked, “When are we going back there?”

“We’ll go to the Pentecostal Church when things are real bad,” replied Doreen.

In the Kitchen, Helen asked, “How was it?”

Carol turned, grabbed the lapel of her jacket with one hand, raised the other toward Heaven and in the fervent dialect she had heard that morning, proclaimed, “Friends and neighbors, I come forward today to share something with you and that something is JEEEEEESUUUUUUSSSSS!”

“There’ll be no more o’ that young lady,” said Helen. After Carol went to change her clothes, Helen looked at Doreen and asked, “Where does she get this stuff?”

Doreen shrugged as she reached under the sink.

COWGIRL CAROL

Since her arrival at the mansion, Carol had become addicted to the westerns on the television, all of them, the Lone Ranger, Hop-a-long Cassidy, Gene Autry, and Roy and Dale included. Doreen had spotted the little cowgirl outfit at Lear's Clothing Store two weeks before Carol's birthday and had bought it right then - gun, boots, hat, and all.

Doreen also baked a cake and made a big to-do, and just at the right moment, she laid the large package in front of Carol. While Helen raised a fuss about the money, Doreen watched Carol go into an apoplexy of delight and wonder. Her little hands shook as she stood in her chair and kicked off her clothes and began to dress in the new outfit. Doreen helped her button the western style blouse, then showed Carol how to pull the skirt over her head. When it was buttoned and zipped, Carol pulled the vest on and Doreen helped her strap on her pistol. Her eyes looked up as the little red straw cowgirl hat was placed firmly on her head as though she were the center of a royal coronation. She ran her hands down the white and red dress and over the brightly embroidered cactus, lariats, and pony. Carol was a very happy cowgirl.

Then, Doreen handed Carol two more packages. Carol's hands trembled as she opened the first parcel; a pair of red and white-fringed gloves and white cowgirl boots. The second was a bag with a pole hanging out.

When Carol's eyes fell on the small horse's head, she knew just what to do. She was off- straddling the pony, yanking the reins and trotting toward the big mirror in her aunt's room to get the full effect.

Helen started again, "Aunt Doreen, it's just too much now, just too much."

"I just had more fun than that child, just a-watchin' her. I ain't got nothin' ta' spend my money on and what I do with my money, I reckon, is my own damn business."

"OK ol' woman," Helen answered, "Just don't spoil her."

"I don't think that's possible," Doreen answered.

Carol stood in front of the big mirror, first waving this hand and then the other, to watch the fringe move. Then, she wiggled her butt a little and watched the fringe on the skirt move.

After trying several poses and pantomimes, Carol began her draw practice. Her method was crude at first; however, she found if she held the holster with one hand and pulled the gun with the other hand, it worked pretty slick.

Finally, feeling confident, Carol walked toward the mirror, very slowly, from across the room. She watched herself closely in the mirror. There she stood, one toe forward and one out, one hand on her hip, the other resting comfortably on the six-shooter. Her eyes wandered over the embroidered western scenes, then the fringe, then the bullets in the holster belt, resting finally on the tin star pinned to her chest.

When the fantasy was properly fueled, Carol jumped astride her pony and circled the room until the cadence of her heels really did sound like a horse. Then, she was off to the kitchen to give Aunt Doreen another big hug.

Doreen had just finished her second bourbon and coke. It was something Doreen did on special occasions and in case of illness, anxieties, odd church experiences, and other woes. She was considering reaching under the sink for just a bit more of that Old Crow.

When Carol and the pony galloped into the kitchen, Doreen was bending over to gather up the wrapping paper from the floor. As Carol galloped directly to Aunt Doreen to deliver the hug, the hard horse's head quite strategically reached the old woman's backside first.

Doreen squalled, as she remained bent while she paddled air to get away from the horse's head. She momentarily caught balance in the doorway to the dining room and stopped. As she tried to quickly regain balance, the horse's head struck pay dirt again. More havoc ensued insuring Doreen yet another trip to the sink.

Wells ventured toward the kitchen the following morning. It may have been to discuss the household business, or maybe to try to maintain control of his domain or maybe he just missed seeing

Doreen as much as he had before Helen arrived. Regardless, Wells wandered about thinking until he had enough household business in mind to merit a visit to the kitchen.

Carol, like many a good cowgirl, slept in her new clothes. At daybreak, she fed and watered her new pony in the round white watering trough in the bathroom. Then, she decided to ride on down to the kitchen to see if there was any grub.

Again, she circled the room, perfecting the cadence of a horse's hooves, and she was off. Upon entering the kitchen, Carol spied the tall old stranger standing over Doreen. Carol jumped off the pony, pulled the gun and jammed it into to the stranger's leg and yelled in her piercing voice, "Stick 'em up, Mister!"

Wells spun around, yelped a bit, and almost fell.

"SHE SCARED THE BEEJESUS OUT OF ME!" he shouted. Then, suddenly it all came back to him . . . the child!

Carol looked up smiling, "Don't worry, Aunt Doreen'll get some bluing and clean the beejesus right outa them britches." Both Helen and Doreen apologized to Wells as they reined in the child and tried in vain to suppress their laughter.

Wells walked toward the library, pausing occasionally to look over his shoulder. "What have I done to myself? A child! What in the hell have I done?" He now remembered Doreen and Helen mentioning a child. He supposed he had just chosen to ignore it. His daily agenda began and immediately consumed him. Through the day, he reflected on the events in the kitchen. As the day wore on, he smiled a bit.

A week later, Wells sat in his study debating whether it was safe to try another visit to the kitchen.

AN ENLIGHTENING EXPERIENCE

Carol had to go to the bathroom. Usually, it wasn't a problem. This morning, however, her mom was in their bathroom, so Carol ran to Doreen's bathroom. It too was occupied. Carol knew there was another bathroom somewhere down the hall, but would her mom or her Aunt Doreen be close enough to help her if she needed it, Carol was out of options. She really had to go. She raced about the main floor looking in each room. Finally, under the stairs, she found the powder room.

After her business was complete, Carol gained enough confidence to try the toilet paper by herself. She had seen her Mom do this enough times. First, she wound the paper around her hand, then she gave it a quick jerk…but it didn't break off. Instead several more feet of paper rolled off. Carol, still holding herself with her left hand to keep from falling into the big bowl, wound the loose paper onto her arm then gave another big yank.

With a good twenty feet of toilet paper now off the roll, the paper was wound up to her elbow. She gave it one last yank. Ten more feet of paper reeled off the roll. Angrily, Carol grabbed the paper with her now fully bound arm and tried to bite it in two. This motion pulled the paper tighter around her arm.

That is the moment Carol decided to go for help. Down the long hall she shuffled, her arm bound in paper and her panties at her ankles. The going was slow as she moved toward the kitchen.

"Well I never…"

Carol looked up to see Mr. Wells looking down at her and seeming somewhat disgusted. She smiled up at him. Wells was determined to help this distressed child. He picked Carol up and, with his arms stiffly and fully extended, marched with her to the kitchen.

Doreen and Helen sat drinking coffee. They sat up, shocked, as Wells entered the room and placed Carol in front of her mother. "Lady, it's no place of mine to tell you how to raise your child, but the idea of such a small child alone in a bathroom is bad enough, but to leave a child with a broken arm alone is completely out of my understanding." Wells meant to continue, but Helen's expression had changed from shock to surprise and, as he finished his tirade, she and Doreen burst into laughter. Wells was infuriated and was about to launch into another round of lecture when Helen reached down and started tearing the toilet paper off Carol's arm.

Wells stuttered, "Well! . . . oh for heaven's sake!" Then, embarrassed, he left the kitchen grumbling. As he walked down the hall, his mumbles gradually turned to quiet chuckles. Later, as he sat in his well-ordered library, he contemplated whether this girl was a calamity or a comedienne. He wasn't sure yet, but he was sure life sure was more interesting than it used to be.

HOLLERWEEN IN OTTER HOLLER

Carol didn't think Halloween was that big of a deal. Of course, she didn't remember that much about it. Back in the holler, all Halloween amounted to was a bowl of popcorn and some pranks. Oh, there was the usual bag of cat shit on fire on someone's porch or a tossed egg or two. And then there were the Cayne boys.

The Caynes were brave and brazen, but they only found these qualities in a bottle of their daddy's moonshine. So far this Halloween night, they had beat up the Freemont boy, lit the gas tank on ol' Mrs. Windon's washing machine, and axed the floor out of the Devericks' outhouse.

Finally, the brothers got to Helen's little house. Tom Cayne, the oldest, knew that Ted was overseas and the liquor helped him with the rest. He threw a sheet over his head and stood in front of the door.

"Trick or treat in thar," he howled.

Helen glanced through the curtain at the staggering sheet holding an oil lantern. "Oh boy," she said.

She quickly got her coat, walked past the sleeping Carol, and stepped through the door, quietly pulling it shut. "What do you boys want?" she asked.

The sheet staggered forward. "Why, I'm the ghost of Hollerween and I give people what they need. Tonight, I'm gonna give you what you need, little lady." Then he pantomimed the act of love. The hunching sheet was a sight.

Almost to herself, Helen responded, "Sometimes, I give people what they need too." She shifted her coat to one side and her slender arm raised the old Colt hog-leg pistol. The long Colt revolver bucked in her hand like a fire-breathing bull.

When the gun was empty, Helen stepped into the living room and dropped the revolver on the couch, grabbed up the Winchester thirty-caliber rifle and returned to the porch. Helen took a couple of final shots above the sheets as they disappeared up the road.

"Trick or treat, my ass." She whispered.

Halloween was over in Otter Hollow.

HALLOWEEN IN OAK HILL

Shortly after her birthday, Carol was presented with a white mask to go with her cowgirl outfit. Carol and Helen were given directions to follow and with an A&P bag in hand, Carol was off for her very first-ever trick-or-treat outing. The two of them had never had so much fun together. Carol and her mom giggled at the sight of every jack o' lantern, scarecrow, and costume. Meanwhile, Doreen stayed behind to hand out candy and, because of the monotony of it all, she began to sip on a pint of Old Crow in between goblin visits.

So, Helen had a good time, Carol had a good time, and Doreen had a real good time. Wells, staring out of his bedroom window, had a good time too, watching the heathen and her mama and the knee-slapping candy giver on his porch.

As Carol and her Mother marched up the street, Wells spotted the red kerchief tied around Carol's neck.

"My word! Rednecks under my own roof," he said. He laughed as he walked away from the window.

T.G. LOOSENS UP

The following Monday, Wells cautiously entered the kitchen for the weekly business meeting. Not knowing when Carol might burst in, Wells refused to be seated for this meeting. Doreen sat at the large red and gray melamine table and watched him pace while she busied herself with a basket of clothes and a shaker bottle full of starch.

"… and, in conclusion, Doreen, to help you occupy this child, she may use some selections from the library, provided she is taught to respect the books."

Doreen stared. She was rarely allowed to even clean the library, let alone borrow a book.

"The child must ask for each book specifically, as there are some valuable first editions," he added.

"Uh, yes, sir, of course."

"That will be all."

"I'll be damned!"

"Beg your pardon?"

"That's awful nice of you, Mr. Wells."

"I know." Wells could never resist his own brand of humor.

"And I'll darned sure to show her how to handle them books."

"Good."

For three days, Doreen and Helen coached Carol on proper library and book etiquette. On the fourth day, they took her into the library to acclimate her to this 'hallowed environment.'

Carol marched around the room staring at the rows of oak shelves and glass doors. She then glanced at the magazines. Finally, she parked in front of *The Encyclopedia of Natural History*. She wasn't fascinated with the subject at all. The book just happened to have pictures.

Carol spotted one picture in particular and stared at it for a minute. Then, she marched through the door, across the hall, and into Mr. Wells' office.

"Mr. Wells, can I, uh … may I use the book with the lizard?"

"I believe that's a din-o-saur," he replied slowly enunciating each syllable.

"Who's Din-ah, your cou-sin?" she replied as slowly.

"You may read the book, Carol."

"Can't read! Gotta look at the pictures," she announced in a matter-of-fact fashion.

"Just help yourself…"

"Thanks"

"You're welcome"

The old man, who could stay up for three days without sleep during labor negotiations, was suddenly exhausted.

A TRIP TO MARKET

The following morning Doreen and Carol backed the Chevy out and drove down the hill to Prince's Market to gather a few necessities. Doreen wouldn't drive the mile and a half beyond Prince's to the A&P unless she was really serious about shopping. She walked down the aisles and eventually found everything she had written on her list. Carol also found several necessities for herself, but Doreen kept putting them back. Finally, she promised Carol some Bazooka bubblegum if she behaved.

At the checkout counter, Doreen put the groceries on Wells' account, then, separately paid for the bubble gum, her cigarettes, and other personal items.

Carol was suddenly thrilled she had worn her badge and gun, for in front of her waiting to check out was none other than Coy Browning, Oak Hill's part-time policeman.

Coy had become a state trooper at the age of 20 and had served 37 years and retired. Now, 61 years old, Coy could still handle a man half his age. To fight boredom and augment his state pension, Coy worked evenings and weekends with the Oak Hill police force. Coy was happy to stay busy and the Oak Hill chief of police was happy to have a seasoned professional. Policing had picked up since the county had voted out the temperance statute. Fayette County was no longer dry. In fact, it had become downright damp.

Coy stood at the register to pay for the two-pound bag of coffee and the powered sugar doughnuts. He wore Oak Hill's regulation Army Navy surplus khaki slacks and shirt and polished black heavy-heeled shoes. Coy refused to wear the policeman's visor-style hat, opting for an old khaki drill instructor style Stetson. It reminded him of his old state trooper uniform.

"Psst! – Psst!"

Coy turned to see where the noise was coming from. As he looked down, Carol threw her coat open to display the badge and gun. Then, she gave Coy a knowing wink. Coy suppressed a chuckle, turned solemnly and saluted Carol. Her eyes lit-up and she returned the salute.

Coy gathered up his groceries and change, nodded to Doreen and Carol, and marched out to the patrol car, smiling.

THE OLD TROOPER

Coy was, by nature, stern-faced enough to make an inexperienced felon confess just by eye contact and make an habitual criminal sweat like he was before his Maker. Standing six foot three and weighing in at two hundred twenty pounds, he wasn't all growl and no-bite either. Few men, young or old, dared cross Coy if they knew him. With Coy, justice was swift and brutal.

The first Saturday night of the miners' vacation, the Riffle Boys came down from Table Rock Holler and decided to try out a new Oldsmobile. They had tried out a car a year before in Beckley and, now, it was worn out. They didn't pay for it, mind you. They just never came back with it, and no lawman would ever go to Table Rock Holler for a measly car. Another time, the Riffles took the salesman with them. They threatened him and tied him to a tree for a little torture that would ensure his silence. No charges were ever filed.

The Riffles had old Claude Jenkins up against the fender of a new Oldsmobile when Coy spotted them. Coy switched off the lights and drifted onto the soft grass shoulder just beyond the car lot. He pulled out a twelve-gauge, short-pump riot gun and walked quietly behind the used trucks.

Geronimo Riffle held the revolver against old Claude's head. Moses and Sinks Riffle were trying to hot-wire the new "Rocket 88" and L. T. Riffle stood giggling beside Geronimo.

Coy had previously encountered the Riffles and knew their reputation. He couldn't figure out if L.T. was a man or a woman. He always did a double take when L.T. appeared, L.T. being slender, small and effeminate with a man's clothing and hair. L.T. was also known to be as mean as the rest of the family, however, that wasn't the issue this evening.

Coy had crept close enough to make a move. He took three long strides, stroked the butt of the shotgun into Sinks' forehead, slammed the hood down on Moses, and cracked L.T.'s temple with the gun barrel. He then buried the gun in the soft flesh of Geronimo's chin.

"Give me an excuse, any excuse will do."

Geronimo chuckled and lowered his pistol, then dropped it to the ground. He smiled and started to issue a threat, a threat that was never finished. Coy full-stroked a right cross to Geronimo's chin. He fell back against the car, dropped to his knees, then collapsed face-first into the gravel.

When it came to the law, Coy was all business and business was usually good.

Like most West Virginia State troopers, Coy had suffered through his share of transfers until accumulating enough seniority to provide some leverage in placement. Troopers could be transferred anywhere in the state with only a moment's notice. After eight years, the transfers slowed down and that's when Coy came to Taylor County.

He was stationed at the detachment in Pruntytown. It was here he met his one true love. Irene Harper was the dispatcher and secretary for the Pruntytown detachment, and she was life's perfect match for Coy Browning. She liked hot black coffee in the morning and a shot of straight Jack Daniels in the same cup at the end of the day. Coy liked the same.

It had been an especially busy Friday. After the second shift had left for their respective patrols, Coy and Irene sat, sipping their evening mash and making small talk. Irene pulled a Pall Mall from the pack and lit up. She stood and walked toward the small kitchen, bending over to pick up a scrap from the floor. "Damn!" whispered Coy.

After his fourth cup of 'Jack', Coy garnered the nerve to try to speak. "Miss Harper, I believe you're built like a Roosevelt sponsored WPA brick outhouse."

"Officer Browning, I believe Ol' Mister Jack Daniels done give you a mouth to write some mighty big checks with, boy."

"Frustrated's all."

"I can cure that," she said

After an hour and a half in the holding cell and the weekend at her apartment, their wedding three weeks later seemed only natural. And they had thirty-two good years together, but her time had come and gone. Now he missed her dearly.

After that, Coy came to settle here in Oak Hill. It was his last assignment as a trooper and since he had no roots, he had stayed.

A THANKSGIVING VISIT

Carol was getting excited about Thanksgiving. After her Halloween experience, the mention of a holiday excited her to an almost intolerable level, Also, this Thanksgiving would be her first visit with her dad at the hospital since their move to Oak Hill. She didn't know him that well, but she figured he must be special because her mom got awful nervous when his name came up.

Doreen bought Carol a watercolor set and she painted everything in sight as bright as the autumn leaves including the leaves, and the white walls on Wells' Coupe de Ville. It took three steel wool pads for Doreen and Carol to restore those tires to their natural whiteness.

Carol loved autumn leaves raked in piles in the lawn. She not only painted them, she rolled in them, jumped in them and sometimes she just laid in them.

As Doreen sat at the kitchen window, peeling potatoes she looked up and started scanning the yard for Carol. While doing this, she saw Wells coming up the walk with the evening paper. When he passed the leaf pile, Carol bolted up out of the leaves and yapped like a pup.

"Oh, Jesus Pete," Wells shouted as he fanned the paper in an attempt to leave the ground it seemed.

"Nope, it's just me – Carol."

Wells grinned out loud and proceeded up the walk.

Studying the look of amusement on his face, Doreen knew the old man had adjusted to having Carol around. Doreen didn't know whether Well's had suddenly realized how much enjoyment came from children or whether he was simply becoming childish himself. Then, she had the same thoughts about herself.

BIT O' ANXIETY

Later that evening, as she cleaned her own room, Helen thought again about the upcoming Thanksgiving outing. She was growing nervous about the trip to Beckley to visit Ted. Her work and Carol occupied these days, long with hope and anxiety. Thank God.

Ted was calmer these days, but the drugs made him seem worse than he was. He would hold out his arms at times in the posture of a small child reaching. Helen had coached Carol to not hug her father. She feared he would hurt her. Carol would talk to him slowly and softly just like her mother, telling him everything as he sat patient, wide-eyed and smiling.

Carol's stocking feet sliding into the room brought her back to reality.

"Hey, Mom, I think you better come and help Aunt Doreen. She's movin' the wabbit ears agin and she's down there callin' the television a sons-a-bits." The stocking feet hammered the floor several times before traction was possible and the child scurried toward the stairs. Helen smiled and followed.

WHO'S GOT THE MARBLES?"

Monday morning, Wells made the trip to the kitchen. The household affairs of the week were a mere repetition of the previous Monday with the exception of Thanksgiving. Wells knew that Helen and 'The Heathen' (his new nickname for Carol) were going to visit the husband. He also knew that if it snowed, the trip would be a struggle, so he did the only honorable thing. He called his sister in Beckley and invited himself to Thanksgiving dinner. This trip to the kitchen was simply to arrange seating for the trip in his Cadillac.

"I've been invited to have Thanksgiving dinner with my sister in Beckley and I'll drive us all down on that morning. We'll leave about eight and it shouldn't be too tough a trip. To help occupy the child, Carol will ride in the front with me," he said. It was not an invitation, just an announcement. He proudly nodded to the kitchen gathering as gesture of his humanity and headed for his office.

As the office door closed, Doreen rocked her head down and then cocked it to one side facing Helen and said, "I don't much think it no more. Now, I just know it. The man has lost his damn marbles."

"I can fix that," Carol whispered to herself. They were going to the store and she'd just see if she could fix him up.

WHAT MARBLES?

A while later, Carol practically towed Doreen into Prince's Market. Once inside, Doreen cut the heathen loose. Carol knew her way around the store and the Princes were at ease to let Carol wander while Doreen shopped unencumbered for the moment.

Doreen had only a few items in her basket when she heard the little voice.

"Hey Mister Prince, where do you keep the marbles?"

Prince replied," Why Carol, they're over there beside them playing cards. Do you like to play marbles?"

Doreen was half-sprinting down the aisle toward the counter.

"Oh no, they're not for me, they're for ole Mister Wells", she answered. "You see he lost his marbles an' I just figured on helpin' him git'em back"

Doreen turned the corner and grabbed Carol's hand and led her around to the next aisle and furiously explained that that subject was not to be talked about in public. "Now, tell Mr. Prince that you're sorry."

"Why?"
"I'll tell ya' later "
" Oh."
Then Doreen whispered privately to the child. Carol nodded as she listened to her Aunt's special instructions.
Carol walked up to Mr. Prince and said, "On second thought, Mister Prince, "How about some ice-cream?"

" What about the marbles?"

"What marbles?"

"The ones you was just askin' about, . . . oh, never mind,

what kinda ice-cream do you want?" he growled.

" Choclate, didn't ya hear me?"

"Well, if you said it I guess I didn't!" he snapped.

He started to ask what size cone when he looked up to see a former state trooper on one end of the counter and the meanest housekeeper in Oak Hill on the other. Instead he piled the cone high, stuck a cherry on top and squeezed out a little smile as he handed the cone to the nerve wrecker before him.

Coy backed away, happy that the gruff storekeeper had wisely opted to concede the debate, regardless of the topic. He enjoyed his visits to the market but this wouldn't stop him from correcting a crotchety old storekeeper if the need arose.

With his shopping complete, Coy headed for the register to check out. As he passed the cards and comic books he casually reached over and grabbed a bag of marbles; then as he passed the now chocolate-faced Carol, and Doreen, he put on the sternest face he could muster, dropped the marbles into Doreen's basket, then nodded and said, "Ma'am." He saluted Carol (to which she immediately saluted in return) then left.

He laughed all the way home.

"Are they the right kind of marbles?" Carol asked.

"Kinda good-lookin' somebody," Doreen answered quietly as she watched the wiry limbed, chiseled faced ex-trooper exit the store.

After they left the store, Doreen and Carol drove around just long enough for Doreen to deprogram the child.

Later that day, poor Ol' Mr. Prince looked at his wife and said, "I use to like kids, I'm almost sure of it."

ANGELS WE HAVE HEARD ON HIGH

That afternoon, as Doreen started peeling the supper potatoes, she took a call from her old friend, Lucille Lewis. Lucille always made Doreen feel good about herself, almost as if she were born of royalty and there had been some horrible mistake at the hospital, and well, naturally, Lucille was one of Doreen's oldest and truest friends.

After exchanging greetings and other cordialities, Lucille began.

"Why, Doreen, I'm in such an awful fix and only you and you alone can save me."

"Well now just you calm yourself, Hon," replied Doreen. "How can I help you? Just tell me".

This was easier than ol' Lucille planned. "Oh, Doreen, to make a long story short, I'm in charge of the Christmas pageant at Oak Hill Baptist again this year. Well, I do it every year. And last year, well, we had just enough angels and this year we're short a few and well, I hate to impose not knowing if your niece is already in a pageant in your own church, but could you find your way free of conscience to help an old friend and let us borrow your little niece for our pageant? Oh, please?"

"Well, Lucille, you just honor me. You really do."

"Oh, thank you so much", smiled Lucille through the phone lines. She continued,

"Practice is Friday evening at seven sharp – now write it down and don't forget. We'll talk about the angel costumes that you'll be sewing when you get there. And, once again, God bless you and thank you, thank you, you dear, dear woman."

Doreen hung up the phone and the more she thought about it, the more pleased she was to bail out Lucille and her fellow parishioners.

THE EPPSES

The Epps girls had grown up fifty yards from the Dutch King Coal Company's Tipple No. 4. Their father, Lemuel Epps, liked to call himself the Tipple Master and at other times, Tipple Supervisor. He possessed a strong pride in working his way up to this position.

The pay wasn't bad but the fringe benefits were questionable at best. First, from nineteen years of the constant churning of chains and belts and the grind of the crusher, Lemuel was as hard of hearing as a fish. Second, from nineteen years of breathing coal dust fourteen hours a day, Lemuel had no lungs to speak of. Also, about ten years before, the boys who picked the sulfur gobs, steel pieces, and other junk off the belt leading into the crusher, had missed four sticks of dynamite. When the dynamite hit the crusher, it blew the top into the floor of the control room, shattering Lem's left leg and damaging the rest of him as well. Lem considered himself fortunate though. The three Washington brothers and one-legged Charlie working the belt line had all been killed.

Another benefit of Lem's job was the free housing provided by the company. It was only a fifty yard walk to work but the natural flow of the wind dropped that coal dust right on their house.

Lem could run but he could not hide. So, he shared his poor lungs with his wife, April and his eldest daughter, Alice May. They were as consumptive as thirty year deep-mine drill operators. April's lungs were so poor, she could no longer sleep laying down. Alice May's condition gave her a distended chest and only a whisper for a voice.

Mark Watson drove a double-B model Mack tandem-axle dump truck at the tipple. He was an ambitious man, usually grabbing the first and last loads of the day. Mark had been fond of Alice May in school and even now when he saw her he would blow the air horns, or wave, or if time allowed he'd just stop and talk a bit. Well, Marks translation of Alice's distended posture and her whispery voice was purely sexy. Through his stammering and stuttering, he eventually asked for a date.

When her mom died, it seemed right for Alice May to marry Mark. Alice May announced her plans one evening after supper. Her only reluctance in the matter was what was to become of her little sister, Sheila.

"Daddy, I know how busy you are up at the tipple an' all, an' if it'd be a help, Sheila can come live with me an' Mark." Her father didn't have time to respond.

"Well big sister, maybe you ain't the only one with a weddin' plan", Sheila added.

"Who you gonna marry, Sheila?" Alice May inquired, stunned by the revelation.

"You'll know soon enough", she replied with a childish sneer.

Alice May looked to her father for any kind of support, but the old man just seemed relieved. Nothing Alice May said could dissuade her.

Two weeks after Alice May and Mark took up housekeeping, Sheila married her mystery man. Then it became evident why it was kept a secret. Ernest "Butch" Everett, an uncommon white trash dozer mechanic, twelve years her senior, was her surprise beau.

Butch and Sheila moved into a Yankee-framed shanty on his grandfather's farm and within a month he had established a regimen of working, drinking, and beating his wife, as required. Sheila seldom saw Alice May, being either too beaten up or drunk to venture out.

Alice May and Mark had a short and joyful marriage. In the third year Alice May had a son. The pregnancy and delivery took its toll on the already fragile Alice May. She weakened further, but Mark doted on both mother and child. When he wasn't in his truck, Mark was caring for their every need and desire.

Two years later, during a fierce snow storm, Mark pulled over to help old "Catfish" Wilson put chains on his truck and don't you know, that son of a bitch ran over poor Mark and killed him.

Sheila showed up for the funeral eight and a half months pregnant and with a hardhearted demeanor. Sheila's view of Alice May was as equally bleak. Alice May's breathing was now a series of sighs and her words now had taken on a breathless economy. It was the first time the sisters had been together since their father's funeral two and a half years before.

They both said their "hi's" and "how are you's." Then, they sat in front of the casket and shook a few hands talking between.

"Your ol' man still givin' ya a rough time," Alice May whispered.

"Naw, I givin' em the cure."

"How's that?"

"Aw, he smacked me there one night after I got pregnant, an' then he went to the outhouse for a sit down, an' I fired that twelve gauge at the door, just ta' scare em' a bit an' don't ya know that ol' poplar door is so soft, why I just peppered the hell outta' him." Sheila continued. "I ain't gonna say he respects me more, but he ain't drawed back since."

Alice May smiled at her still ornery little sister, and Sheila's smile was returned through broken teeth.

After the service, and then sometime later, Alice May and Sheila sat alone waiting. Butch would be along with the truck soon.

"Sheila honey, I want ya' to listen real hard," Alice May whispered. Sheila felt the urgency in her voice and moved closer.

Alice May continued, "Mama come to me in a dream last night, an' well, Sheila, I know I ain't long for this world." Sheila stared back at her sister, not knowing how to respond at first.

The day had been taxing. Alice May sat in front of a window with the setting sun to her back and Sheila could see her frail, blanched silhouette through the light nightshirt – the appearance was ghostly. The only thing that made her seem alive were the dark circles about her eyes and the perspiration that covered her face and body.

"Sheila, you gotta promise me..."

"You ain't gonna die, Alice May, dammit ta hell! You're just..."

" Just promise."

" Alright but..."

"You take my baby."

Sheila had watched her mother and father die this same way. She knew that Alice May's time was near.

"Now.."

"Sheila, I can't lay down without choking. "

"Why don't ya go to that clinic up in Barbour County like Aunt Maby did?"

"Honey, Aunt Maby's dead an' I'm outta time. Say you'll do it, an' don't let that son of a bitch lay a hand on him." She whispered between gasps.

"OK, I'll do it."

The GMC pulled up to the gate and the horn sounded. Sheila followed the rock steps down the steep bank to the roadway and stood beside the truck with folded arms.

"Well, woman are ya' gonna get in?"

"Alice Mays gonna be needin' me here for a spell." Sheila said.

"She'll hafta get used to being alone some time, now dammit get in the truck," Butch snapped.

Sheila glared back. She put her hands on her hips and stepped down in the road beside the truck. " She's dying," she said only loud enough for him to hear. "Now, I'm stayin' on an' you can drop me off some clothes here tomorrow, an that's that."

A year sooner would have found a battered wife beside Butch on the way home. He simply glared back, nodded, and drove off.

Later that evening after Sheila had fed the baby and put him down for the night, she helped Alice May wash and get into her nightshirt. Then she propped her up with pillows on the couch and found her too exhausted to even talk. Just being away from Butch made her feel decent again. She stooped to give her big sister a hug goodnight and they held each other for the longest, most wonderful time.

Two weeks later, Alice May was buried next to Mark. The next day, Sheila gave birth to her own baby boy.

Over the years, Butch made a few attempts at parenting the dull son of Mark and Alice May. Butch turned out to be as cruel a parent as he had once been a husband. When Little Mark was six, Sheila came in from the garden to find Butch whipping the boy with his miner's belt. She scooped up the child and raised her finger as though leveling another rifle. "If you ever touch my sister's child again, I'll take the wind out o' your sails an' you know damn good an' well I can do it." Butch feigned laughter and mockery, but he never touched the child again. He didn't have to.

ARTIE

For all the evil locked in the soul of Butch Everett, it came back in spades in the form of his son. Artie Everett was a beautiful baby with a beautiful smile. But as he aged he became somewhat like a dog that wags its tail when you pet it, then as you walk away, it strikes. Yes, Artie Everett was a heel-biting son of a bitch if ever one lived. If he could lie, cheat, or steal to get what he wanted without the least honest effort, then that was the path he took.

Artie always included cousin Mark, from the time they were children, and still, sometimes to have a good listener, sometimes as an unwitting partner in crime, and sometimes to be the butt of his sick jokes.

Sheila's description of Mark was simply, "Well, he's kind of a dull boy." If the truth were known, Mark was just a sweet and mildly retarded boy. His mental state might have come from a mother who couldn't take in enough oxygen during her pregnancy, it may have come from malnutrition, or it may have come from Butch's 'private' beatings in the early years.

Now, Mark just hung out with Artie. Artie easily convinced Mark that his place in life was to help him at the strip mine, keep house in their little rented shack, and get out when Artie showed up with one of his drunken girlfriends.

At the strip mine where he worked, Artie ran a small Ingersoll-Rand drill and handled all of the dynamite and other explosives. Artie's favorite prank was to short fuse a shot and, as they walked from the hole, Artie would tell the laborers how many seconds they had before it went off, sending his panic-stricken crew running for cover. It finally got to the point where the only one who would work with Artie was Mark.

Although Artie was the best shooter around, sooner or later he rubbed every body the wrong way and eventually Artie and Mark worked for almost every coal operator in the area. Finally they were hired at Wells Mountain Coal. Because of the higher pay and benefits, Artie worked a little harder at his behavior. Besides, this outfit used caps and wire and Artie felt more like a professional.

After two years his professionalism abandoned him. He thought he was just too valuable to be let go for simply insulting his foreman, but he was wrong. On November 6th he was fired. On November 7 Artie got his severance pay, got a bottle, got on a drunk, and stayed there until November 22. He sobered up enough to visit his dad at the VA Hospital in Beckley, on Thanksgiving.

AT LONG LAST . . . BECKLEY

The Thanksgiving trip was an affair to remember.

The Cadillac had been serviced, cleaned, and waxed for the trip. The ladies were equally prepared. They had arranged a portable feast, in hope of sharing it with Ted. Doreen had even bought Carol a new winter coat and hat. Helen couldn't tell if Doreen was dressing Carol up or if this amounted to a 'hush payment' for sins Carol and Doreen happened to commit together. Nonetheless, Carol did certainly look cute in red and blue plaid.

As they loaded and entered the already warming car, Wells restated the seating arrangement.

"Carol will sit in the front with me." It was inferred that Helen and Doreen could sit wherever they wanted. Wells gave Carol the final "Co-pilot" instructions as to the operation of the radio, heater, power windows and so on.

Carol enjoyed being second in command and due to the forty-five degree weather, she was finally convinced to keep the windows closed. After several more minutes of heater adjusting and radio tuning, Carol settled into a tourist/sightseer mode with the occasional interrogatories of, "What's that?" and " How long till we get there?" Doreen passed an occasional pumpkin cookie to help Carol fight boredom. No one else dared eat in the Cadillac.

Wells pulled up in front of the hospital at 9:45. He looked at Helen and said, "Why don't you and Doreen see what arrangements you'll have to make for your meal while Carol and I tour the lobby."

"That would be a big help," she replied. Wells could read the anxiety in her eyes.

Carol had been here before and she took great pains in giving her good friend, Mr. Wells the "tour of the lobby." She showed him the flag, the bronze plaque, and the water fountain, where he had to pick her up. Then, Carol made Wells lean over and she told him how the nurse's hat looked like the screen at the drive-in movie.

About then, Doreen came out of the elevator looking rather puzzled.

"Well, I swear. He seems like he's completely normal now. It's kinda spooky. Anyway it's all set. We'll visit a spell and then we'll eat some lunch and then we'll be ready for when you come by later to pick us up," she said.

Carol joined her mother while Wells helped Doreen unload the food and as they carried it toward the activity hall he handed her a card and said," My sister's telephone number is written there on the back. I'll be here as planned at 2:30 unless I hear from you before. You wouldn't be interrupting anything. In fact, you would probably be doing me a favor."

"I appreciate that and every thing else you've done today. I really do," said Doreen.

He followed Doreen into the Activities Hall and toward the table where Helen sat. Carol was tight against her right leg and before her sat her husband, Ted. As Wells sat the basket down on the table, Ted rose and extended his hand.

"Thank you for the kindness you been showin' to my family, sir," Ted spoke as slowly and as deliberately as an old man. Wells also noted the boy had as many lines in his face as he. Ted moved almost cautiously as though he was in a fragile state but on the surface he appeared wiry. Ted stood a slender six feet even with a shock of straight brown hair combed toward his back. His chiseled face had the pallor of a man who'd been denied sunlight, but Wells noticed how he kept his eyebrows raised as though in a mode of anticipation. He wondered how long they'd been raised and how long they would remain in this state.

Wells, who could read any man at a glance, was vexed. Doreen was right, 'kinda spooky.'

Wells looked at his watch and smiled, "It was nice to meet

you Ted, but I must be running along. I'll be expected. I guess I'll see you ladies again at 2:30."

Ted stared toward the ceiling and exhaled, "You might oughta' make it back here closer ta' 1:00 or 1:30 if ya could. This place gets real busy after that." The flat trembling tone of Ted's voice left no doubt in Wells' mind as to when he should return.

"That would actually be better for my schedule as well. I'll see you then."

As Wells started to walk away, Doreen said, " Oh, I forgot my cigarettes in the car."

After the swinging doors closed behind them, Wells said, "Your cigarettes are in your purse. I saw you put them there."

"That boy gives me the willies," she replied.

"You'll just have to keep your chin up for your niece."

He left her in the Visitors Lounge, knowing full well, the bottle of liquor was already to her lips.

As Wells made his way back to the Lobby, he saw coming toward him, a nurse with such a swagger that she either was completely in charge or she had a slight hip displacement. Wells interrupted her march, "Pardon me, would you be the nurse in charge?"

" Yes sir, may I be of assistance?" snapped the nurse.

Wells glanced at the nametag. SPC.4 I. Davis; Veterans Administration, Beckley, W.Va.

He replied," I was wondering about the current condition of one of your patients."

"Are you a member of the immediate family?" she volleyed.

"Of course."

Wells had interrupted Nurse Iris Davis on her way to the Employees Lounge for her break. He could tell by the way she held her pen between the index and middle fingers that she was ready for a cigarette. She answered as she inched her way the last few yards to the lounge. “Well, what’s his name, hon’?” she inquired.

“Ted McMurfree, he seems different, he…”

“Well, sure he’ll seem different. He’s on a brand new drug. It’s new, it’s powerful, but it certainly has its limitations,” as she finished her sentence, she finally stepped into the lounge, placed the cigarette into her mouth and struck the match in one graceful motion.

Within seconds she calmed and smiled.

“Has electric-shock therapy been considered in this case?” he continued.

“You care for some coffee, hon?”

“No thanks,” he replied.

She finished pouring and mixing hers and with caffeine in one hand and nicotine in the other, only then did she continue. “What we have here is an all-purpose facility. There are many types of VA facilities. There are VA hospitals that specialize in mental patients.”

“How wonderful,”, he replied, “Are there any nearby?”

“The Veterans Hospital in Martinsburg specializes in mental patients. I know what the next question is. Your boy, Ted, simply doesn’t want to go. Said he doesn’t want to be around that many crazy people and besides this is closer to home.” She finished, balancing a cigarette ash as she looked for an ashtray.

“Well, you have certainly been helpful. I really appreciate what you do and for sharing this information,” he replied.

“That’s why they give me the money, hon.”

Wells thanked her again and excused himself. *This is an interesting piece of information* he concluded and vowed to research the matter.

DOING THYME

At times, Wells looked forward to visiting his sister and her family. He always received a warm genuine greeting, as he did this day. They exchanged the usual "how are ya's" and nibbled on olives and celery as the Grand Feast began.

Mike and Edith had three children: Mary Elizabeth, Annette Adele, and Mike Jr. Mary Elizabeth was in her last year of high school and was bright and witty and talented. Although it was rare for females to do so, Wells envisioned law school for her. Annette Adele would forever be a cheerleader and Mike Jr. would always be an asshole. They had to pass it on to someone.

His visits always started in this cordial manner and soon enough, Edith would be putting on airs and Mike would start trying to get insider gossip. Wells was entertained by their efforts.

Wells remembered when they had nothing and when he decided to get out of the truck business, he simply turned it over to his brother-in law and sister. Now every four years, when Wells Mountain Coal replaced its fleet, they bought the trucks from Mike. Most of the time, Wells was treated like an equal or less in their home, but on the year that the fleet was due to be replaced, they seemed to, more or less, really kiss his ass. He visited when he could but on the year of the purchase, he avoided them at all costs.

Dinner was served at 12:15. Mike and Mike Jr. were finished at 12:35. The dinner conversation was restricted to "pass the," " thank you," and "gimme the….". Wells praised the chefs, said his adieus and departed at 12:55. The Mikes, suffering from a severe relapse of turkey narcolepsy, weren't awakened for his departure.

MEANWHILE, BACK AT THE VA…

As Wells' Cadillac rolled through the quiet streets of Beckley and toward the hospital. He toyed with the idea that holidays might just be a lesson in tolerance. He frowned at the thought as he approached the entrance of the hospital, then wondered how they were faring inside.

"Weeeelll, lookie thar yonder a comin'," yelled Artie.

"What? Where?" asked Mark.

"There, dammit! In that boat-sized Cadillac," said Artie loudly again.

Artie and Mark had come to visit his father. Butch had developed "sugar" over the years and it was taking its toll. His eyesight was failing miserably, and now they were starting to take off his toes. Artie thought it best if he drank a few beers before going in to visit his dad. He thought the beer would help him tolerate the visit and possibly get rid of the alcohol-induced headache.

"Who's in that big car, Artie?" asked Mark.

"That's that son-of-a-bitch Wells," spat Artie. "He's the son-of-a-bitch 'at just fired us."

"Why's he here?" asked Mark.

"Dunno but, by damn, I'd like to." The cousins watched as Wells parked the Cadillac and then walked right in front of the truck and into the hospital.

"Artie, I don't think we ever met him," said Mark.

"Don't have to meet a son-of-a-bitch to get food snatched outta yer mouth by him," growled Artie. "I'd like to see how he'd feel if all he had was took away."

Mark started to protest again, but anything he said would be wrong. Whenever Artie drank, everything was someone else's fault and, lately, drinking was all Artie was doing.

"Come on Mark, let's get this over with."

As Wells walked down the hall leading to the Activity Hall,

he saw Doreen leaning against the glass panes in the door, watching the people on the other side, like fish in an aquarium. Wells slowed his pace and approached Doreen quietly. “Are you afraid to go in?” he asked.

“No, but I need a little longer break each time I come out,” she replied.

Wells joined her in viewing the group inside. Helen sat with Ted, who was showing signs of stress. His afternoon was as he’d earlier described it. Carol was playing tag with a group of pajama-clad vets.

One of the younger veterans suddenly began chasing Carol with an all out effort. When she found it impossible to get out of his way, she screamed and broke into a run. Wells quickly sidestepped Doreen and bolted through the door and started toward the melee.

By the time he actually cleared the doorway, he found himself facing Ted. Ted was leading Carol by the hand, over the now unconscious veteran. Ted extended Carol’s hand to Wells, mumbled an apology, and went back to Helen’s side where he sat and lit a cigarette. His eyebrows were no longer raised. Ted’s eyes had become like a cougar staring at those of a domesticated world. It was a cool stare with no fear, only a glint of anxiety.

Carol’s hand trembled as she asked Wells, “Why did that man get mad at me an’ run after me like that?”

“I don’t know Carol. I don’t think he knows either,” Wells answered.

“Why did my daddy kick that man in the head?” she asked again.

“To make him stop I guess.”

“Well, it worked,” she whispered. Carol looked up and whispered, ”Can we go out to the car now?”

Wells approached Helen and Ted to tell them that they were going on to the car. As he walked over, he noticed all of the other people had migrated to the other end of the hall as an orderly tried to rouse the man lying in the corner.

"Carol and I are going on to the car to get sorted out," said Wells.

Carol took a giant step forward and stood beside her mother and smiled at her dad. "Thanks for making that man quit chasing me," she said.

"He'll not be botherin' you again, Carol," Ted replied.

....or anyone else for that matter, thought Wells.

"You can bet the ranch on that, mister," agreed Carol.

Ted turned and smiled at Carol. "You watch the cowboys?" he asked.

"She loves television," Helen answered.

"Andy Devine?" asked Ted.

"That's right, buster," answered Carol again.

"I watch some television, too," said Ted. Then, they just stared at each other, sharing this new common thread. Carol then suddenly hopped forward and gave her dad a big hug. He sat there, motionless, almost cringing, having no idea how to respond to her affection.

Carol buttoned her jacket, tipped her hat and said, "So long partner" ...and with a wave, she was off.

Ted's tired eyes brightened.

As they neared the door leading to the hallway, Wells heard hisses and he and Carol turned to the remaining players from the game of tag. When they caught her eye, they sent little waves, winks, and " bye-byes."

Carol smiled, waved, and blew them a kiss. The mouse-eyed stares followed her down the hall and out of sight.

THE T.G. WELLS TWO-STEP

As they walked down the hallway, Wells decided that, after the events of the afternoon, Carol should learn a little self-defense. As he remembered, his sisters had been rather adept at this maneuver.

He began, awkwardly, "Carol, sometimes a lady, such as yourself, has to defend herself from people like that man your daddy kicked."

"I can't kick that high," she answered.

"Well, you don't have to . . . really," said Wells." There is a place that you can kick a man and it will make him quit chasing you very fast."

"Where?" she asked.

"Well, ah, right, ah, here," Wells said, pointing between his legs, blushing and stammering all the while.

"Like this?" the little foot shot up with the ease and grace of a seasoned ballerina, and connected.

All Wells could do was nod his head. As he leaned against the long green wall in absolute nauseating pain, large tears rolled down his cheeks.

RETREAT

Artie and Mark spent very little time visiting ol' Butch. Mark sat quietly near the radiator, while Artie grilled his father about the effects of losing appendages and limbs.

As he asked the questions, he paced about, stealing everything that wasn't tied down. He took the old man's spending money, a ring, and even his pain medication. He saw a get-well card from his mother. Ten years before, she went to Florida, got a job at G.C. Murphy's, bought herself some teeth, and remarried. She had never returned.

When the amusement wore off, they headed back to the truck. Artie opened a new bottle of bourbon, hoping the hair of the dog would ease the now throbbing headache. He took two long drinks and washed it down with warm beer just as Wells came out of the hospital.

Artie watched Wells approach, holding the child's hand. He also noticed that Wells looked sickly pale and walked with a bit of a limp. When he reached the Cadillac, he opened the driver's door and let the child in, then slowly slid in behind the wheel. He laid his head on the steering wheel.

The bourbon was doing nothing for Artie's headache. He pulled the pill bottle from his pocket and stared. If it made his ol' man forget his pain, it's bound to get rid of this damn headache. He washed the pill down with the warm beer. The afternoon sun washed across his face, and he also laid his head on the wheel.

GOODBYES

As the medication wore away, Ted gradually withdrew into his private world.

"Ted. Ted, look at me," she said softly.

Ted looked up slowly. He was squatting below a window, as if trying to hide. He made eye contact briefly, then covered his eyes. "If I can't get better pretty soon ....you just go on an' make a life for yourself . . . n' Carol," he said.

She stared back angrily, "I ain't never givin' up on you, mister, an' I'll be damn if you're givin' up on us."

He was stunned at her response. He had thought hard on this. He thought this would give her a way out, to get away from him, a new start.

"Don't you love me, Ted?"

"Yea, but . . . " The pause was endless. The pressure was unbearable. The words would not come.

"But what, Ted?" she whispered.

"I just thought it'd be easier for you to jus..."

"Is that what you want, for us to go?"

"No". He cowered even tighter against the wall. Helen, now kneeling beside Ted, reached out and ran her fingers through his hair. As he lowered his head, she felt him trembling.

"I could never leave you. I could never hurt you," she whispered. With her fingers in his hair, she made a tight fist, then slowly pulled his head up to face her once more." You just keep fightin' this, cause I ain't never givin' up on you." Then she closed her eyes and kissed his forehead. When she let him go, his head remained up.

He watched her gather up the basket and walk away. At the door she stopped and turned. She smiled and backed through the door. His mind raced wildly, aimlessly, He was on fire.

HIGH LIKE HANK

Euphoria swept through Artie's entire being. The pain was gone. The high was like none he'd ever felt. It was a partial numbness. Even as he drank now, the alcohol slid down without bite or pain. The pills were a godsend.

Mark sat, mesmerized by the changes washing over his cousin. It was almost like one of those spooky movies at the drive-in. First, Artie was sick and weak and mad, and now he was drunk and happy and crazy.

Artie had watched Wells and the child return to the Cadillac. The next to return was the old lady. She seemed to have trouble walking against the wind, the really confusing part was there wasn't much wind. Then Artie sat up, as Helen came into view. She wore a loose jacket and the dress, though modest, presented her stunningly. Artie whistled quietly across the lower teeth.

"Would you look at that, damn!" he growled. "Now, that's the kinda woman money'll get for ya."

"She's pretty," mumbled Mark.

After she passed the truck, Artie slapped Mark's arm and cried, "Look at the back a' that dress boy; looks like two possums a' fightin' in a gunny-sack."

He roared with laughter, but it was no laugh Mark had ever heard. His chuckles were dispersed like the beating of a drum. Mark was right. Artie had either become ol' man 'Hyde or ol' man Jeckel, he couldn't remember which.

A QUIET RETURN

Wells had promised a stop on the return trip. When he begged off on that promise, Doreen just grinned and nodded. Helen stared out the window and Carol slept with her head on Wells' leg.

Several times, Wells fought off the need to pull over and throw up.

He didn't notice the truck following at a distance on the way home. When they reached Wells' house, Artie stopped the truck, just close enough to view the long driveway. He watched the old woman exit the car and walk toward the house, then the dark-haired vixen carrying the sleeping child. Finally, the old man made his way inside holding on to everything along his way. The Ford pickup pulled away.

When they were out of town, Artie pulled over to make room in his bladder for more beer. He banged and stumbled along to the back of the truck, then held on, as though perched on a cliff. After watching Artie, Wells, and Doreen, Mark wondered if it was common for almost everyone to steal pills at the hospital.

When Artie sat back down and started to drive, he began singing an old 'Opry' tune, but he seemed to get the words all backwards and he added profanity at will to give the tune balance and character.

On the way to their home, Artie and Mark stopped at Butch's house. Mark stood on the porch and shifted from side to side while Artie stumbled about inside searching for more pills and alcohol. He found four bottles of pills and a dust covered, half-bottle of bourbon. Artie washed one of the blue pills down with the bourbon, started the truck, and continued onward into the night.

Later, he sat in a chair, pondering the events of the day. He had trouble focusing on most thoughts, but one idea was indelible. He coveted just about everything ol' Wells had. Oh, he didn't care much about the housekeeper. Everyone knew that mean ol' bitch. Didn't necessarily want any kids, but he sure wanted the mother. And don't forget the money and a fancy car.

As Artie pondered, he wasn't aware that he was mumbling most of his thoughts aloud, incoherently. Mark watched him mumble and contort his face to match the attempted dialog. Mark stared at his cousin, probably the same way he stared at the formaldehyde filled pickle jars at the carnival freak show.

Suddenly Artie quit mumbling, turned his head and smiled, then he nodded in agreement with himself. The fine hairs on Marks body stood on end as he witnessed the madness of his cousin.

DAY IS DONE

While Helen got her daughter ready for bed, Carol chattered unintelligibly about Mr. Wells being mad about something. Helen tucked her in and turned out the light. She then went down the stairs to check on Doreen. The old housekeeper had already kicked off her shoes and curled up for the night.

She passed through the kitchen and noticed the light in Wells office. When she walked down the hallway to turn the light off, she found Wells sitting at his desk. When she stepped into the room, he lifted his ashen face.

"Are you all right?" she asked quietly.

He nodded with a grimace and waved her away without a word.

Later, as she stepped out of the tub onto the cool tile floor, she stared hard into the mirror on the back of the door. As she dried herself, she closed her eyes . . . remembering that rambunctious boy from yesterday. She remembered the feel of the rocks against her feet as she waded into an abandoned millpond hand in hand with Ted in the light of a full moon, as bare as she was now. She remembered the fury that would not allow two country kids to remain children. A quiet moan escaped her throat. She closed her eyes and prayed for his return.

T.G.I.F.

When Wells awoke the following morning, he realized that the soreness from Carol's little kick had more or less localized itself. Everything below his neck ached. He swallowed several aspirin and paced about in an effort to walk off the soreness.

Wells' mood quickly matched his aching groin, destroying his appetite and patience. Wells learned years before to redirect his anger in moments like these. He simply hadn't been angry in a long, long time. He decided to go to the mines and rattle the cages, so to speak.

When he entered the kitchen, Helen looked over from the stove as she prepared breakfast, "Good morning Mr. Wells, and thanks again for yesterday. I'll have your breakfast ready for you in a minute or two."

"That won't be necessary this morning, I have a meeting at the mine," he grumbled. "If you would prepare a thermos of coffee, I'll be going."

"Would you like me ta' make you a nice egg sandwich ta' take along?" she added.

"Just the coffee, please."

A while later, as Helen prepared breakfast for Doreen and Carol, she described Wells' terse mood. Doreen had seen all of Wells moods over the years and this morning, she just didn't seem to care. Carol, on the other hand, knew the reason.

"I reckon it's my fault ol' Mister Wells is mad," she said softly.

"Why honey, what could you have done to make Mister Wells mad," asked Doreen as she blew steam from the heated coffee.

For the next five minutes, Carol explained, in detail, the reason for Wells' demeanor. She even hopped down off of her chair to show them how to do the kick. The two women belly laughed for the better part of ten minutes. Afterward and between spontaneous chuckles, they took turns explaining the power of such a kick and when and to whom she should apply it. Doreen even shared with Carol the name commonly used on that specific piece of anatomy.

Carol, still upset over Mr. Wells' "nuts" and probably weary from the trip, played quietly in front of the television. Occasionally, her solitude was disrupted by an outburst of laughter from the two women in the kitchen.

As planned, Wells' soreness was mistaken for anger at Wells Mountain Coal. He even called his lawyer to the mine. The arrival of the lawyer left all minds to ponder.

The lawyer brought along his new secretary to take notes. Wells noted the beauty of the secretary, but he also noted that she possessed the dry sullen demeanor of white trash. He would have to stay clear of her.

After the standard cut and dried annual reports were reviewed, attorney Peter McKinney looked at Wells and said, "Hell, T.G., we could've handled this at the office," not bothering to mask his disgust.

"I pay enough of a retainer to warrant this type of service and occasionally I request it." The argument was over.

McKinney leaned back in his chair, crossed his legs and looked across the top of his reading glasses reflectively and asked, "What's really bothering you?" he asked.

Wells smiled, looked over at the secretary and asked, "Would you excuse us, please."

Not understanding his request, the secretary started to speak, but McKinney added, "Miss Reed, that will be all. You may wait in the car. Thank you." Her departure was awkward.

A moment after the door closed, Wells spoke, "I would like you to locate the leading people in the field of psychology who specialize in battle shock and whatever cure is recommended. I would like to speak to them within a week. And Peter?"

"Yes sir?"

"I don't know who the new girl is, but until she has proven herself to be beyond reproach, I don't want her near my affairs. Do you understand?"

"Yes, but, she has good references and..."

"I'm not asking you to defend her, I just want this handled discreetly."

"Of course," Peter replied.

As they drove away, Marguerite Reed asked, "What was that all about?"

"Sorry Marguerite, some parts of this job are confidential," he added.

Marguerite Reed hated to be put in her place. She'd made her own way in this world. She had worked her way through all six months of The Summersville Business College, and still, when someone heard the name Reed, she was sent to the car.

"You know best, Peter," she answered smiling. She would simply find out later.

She was baffled by something she had noticed as she walked around the parking lot, smoking her cigarette. In the front seat of Wells' Cadillac was a child's puzzle and toy gun. Oh well, in time she would know all about the famous Mr. Wells.

REAL STRANGE BEDFELLOWS

At nine that same evening, Marguerite made no effort to reach the ashtray. She just held the cigarette out and flipped the ash on the floor. She then rolled over to face her lover. She wore her slip. The rest of her clothes were scattered about as though scattered by a tornado, or worse.

"I don't know what's in that pill bottle, darling, but it sure brings the man out in you, in a nice slow way," said the secretary.

"I'm here ta' please ma'am," answered Artie, "Now tell me more about what you saw up at the mines."

"Like what?" she asked.

"You was sayin' they was toys in the car?"

"Yeah," she continued," there was a jigsaw puzzle and a kid's cowboy gun and things like that."

"What was "he" wantin' with your boss?" Artie staggered about trying to light his cigarette. He wore his boxers and heavy wool work socks.

"Once in a while that damn McKinney jus' clams up like it ain't none o' my damn business." The bourbon and her companion of the evening had helped her free herself of any thing that lent to an intelligent Christian conversation. She had simply reverted back to the coal-hollow whore she was bred to be.

"Ol' Peter McKinney tends ta' walk in when I'm pullin' up my stockins' an' such. He's comin' along, don't worry. I'll let ya' know," she added.

Artie stumbled forward and growled an approval as he caressed the whore's neck.

Artie awoke the following morning not remembering how or when the previous night had ended. He decided, then and there, he'd have to ration his intake of the pills and maybe the alcohol as well. He had invented himself a plan to end up on Easy Street, and he knew he couldn't do it being drunk.

He growled at Mark most of the day. That evening, he drank without the pills. He missed how those pills made him feel. He replaced the euphoria with hard planning, planning for his retirement.

THE TREE

Carol sat, wide eyed, staring at the television. On the screen, a lady was showing the viewers how to decorate 'the tree' for Christmas.

She sat motionless in the front parlor for forty-five minutes. When the show ended and she was sure it wasn't coming back on, she headed for the kitchen like a bee for its nest.

Her mom and Doreen had worried about Carol for a few days, thinking the trip might have been a little too much. She just sat around with a book or in front of the TV. Even Wells worried quietly about Carol, his soreness and limp now a well-etched memory. His worries eased as the screaming short blur passed his office.

She seems normal this morning, he thought.

Carol shot into the kitchen and let out a speech so fast and jumbled it was indiscernible except for the part about Christmas and something about a tree.

Helen spoke "Now, Carol, slow down a little and try again."

Carol caught her breath and composed herself briefly. Her words jumbled once more, in the same fashion.

This time Doreen spoke, "Now hold on there turd-bird. We can't understand what yer a-saying, so slow down a little!"

This time, Carol's presentation came only a little slower and clearer.

"There's a woman on television with a tree with lights and little shiny things and can we do that for Christmas?"

Doreen replied, "Mr. Wells always gets a tree delivered on the twenty second but that's not for about 20 days, honey!"

"Why not now?"
"Because the needles will dry out."

Carol stared at Aunt Doreen for a moment with one brow up. Doreen cringed.

"I helped you and mom with the quilt last month and the needles weren't wet and I don't know what that has to do with this anyway."

"Go ask Mr. Wells," said Doreen glancing at the clock, knowing it was too early for a drink.

Carol took off for Wells' office so quickly, the first few steps in those stocking feet were wasted. Then she got traction.

Wells heard something and looked up in time to see the illuminated face with finger pointing and words just on the tip, slide past his office door.

"Oh dear," he said.

And she stopped sliding and ran into the office, stopping with both hands against the oak desk. Her mouth was open and her head shook with anticipation.

"Mister Wells, there was a woman on TV with a tree with lights on it and shiny things and we need to have one real bad."

"I usually get the tree a few days before Christmas so the needles don't get too dry."

"The one on TV didn't have needles."

Wells didn't understand that phrase but he knew round one was over.

"Carol, the needles grow on the tree."

"Well, we'll just be real careful, not to get stuck. When can we get it?"

It was over. Wells told Carol the tree would come in ten days. She waited while he called the foreman at the mine regarding size and type. He assumed it was over.

"Mr. Wells, where do you keep the lights and other things?"

"Well, we just use some garland and bulbs."

"Where are the lights?"

"We don't have any lights."

"Don't worry, me and Aunt Doreen will get 'em." And she was off. Wells watched the little body slide toward the kitchen and heard her tell her aunt "to warm up the Chevy, we're a going to the store." When he heard Doreen start to protest, he laughed aloud and walked back into his office.

MESSIANIC SEASONAL ILLUMINATION

Coy had enjoyed the little market and his stops were becoming more frequent. Mrs. Prince said Coy was lonely. Her husband said he was just friendly. They were both right.

As Coy strolled the aisles it was like a walking through a museum. He passed a shelf covered with medical supplies that included everything from band-aids to horse liniment and bear grease. The more sophisticated drugs were kept in a glass case on the top shelf. It included sensen, liver pills, and castor oil. In a corner sat an old nail keg filled with fishing poles, kites, and fly swatters. 'Summer' was written on the keg with yellowed chalk.

Every corner held a novel little item to study and in the center of the store was an old "Warm Morning" coal stove with a pipe that went straight up 14 feet and then through the pattern tin ceiling and on through the roof. This morning was cold enough to fire it up and the acrid smell of the coal burning met you as you entered the store and in these parts and on a morning like this it was a smell that meant warmth.

It was a peaceful moment. Coy was studying generations of carbide lamps and coal miner canaries in a spot close enough to the stove to really feel comfortable. Quiet moments like this were rare and Coy regarded them almost as though he were in a cathedral. But, the silent moment was not meant to last.

The voice was like a shift whistle at the mines: loud, clear and shrill. "Good morning, Mr. Prince. Me and my Aunt Doreen come to buy some lights and other decorations. Where is it?"

Coy knew it was little Carol. "What kind of lights, honey? " replied the old storekeeper.

"Why, the kind you hang all over one of them green Christmas trees." Carol stared at the man, as if he were insane.

"Oh, there are some in that box over there by the batteries," muttered the old merchant.

In the box Carol found one string of lights in very poor repair, no bulbs, one box of tinsel and nothing else.

"Well, Mr. Prince, this stuff is no good, where's the rest of it?" asked Carol.

"That's all there is," said Prince.

Coy watched from his perch beside the coal stove as the beaming face turned sour and the little head cocked sideways in sad disbelief.

"But . . ."

"I'm sorry, that's all I've got!" he replied.

Coy could feel himself desperately wanting to shake old Mr. Prince. He waded into the conflict.

"Excuse me," said Coy.

Carol and Doreen offered him just a glance, then returned their hard stares at the old storekeeper.

"Excuse me!" said Coy again, this time a little louder.

Carol gave him a double take, "Oh, hi, Deputy," she whispered sadly.

The need to help ol' Prince with his attitude came back, then he remembered why he had interrupted. Coy looked then to Doreen.

"I was down to the Blue Ridge Rural Power Company paying my electric bill and I looked over in their store where they sell washers and 'frigerators and fans and such and they just got a whole bunch of lights and bulbs and Christmas things in and they're gonna sell 'em there," he offered.

Carol was smiling with her mouth wide open and nodding her head at the same time. She spun half around and slapped Coy's leg, let out a whoop and started to pull Doreen toward the door.

Doreen smiled at Coy and thanked him.

Coy hadn't been this close to Doreen before. He'd always

taken a back seat and just watched the show when he'd seen Doreen and Carol out and about. A couple of times he'd seen the mother.

That Doreen's a pretty good-looking gal, he thought.

He turned to tell Prince goodbye.

"Thanks, Coy. Last time I didn't have popsicles for that kid, ol' Wells called and chewed on me for ten minutes. 'Preciate it."

When Coy drove by the power company on his way back to his apartment, he saw Carol making gestures with her arms and talking wildly and Doreen and the clerk trying to keep up. *What a corker!*

ANTICIPATION

Without realizing it, Wells' life was becoming consumed by Carol and her parents. The events of the morning had proven this fact. He had spent an hour and a half with doctors from Johns Hopkins Hospital and the VA Hospital in Pittsburgh.

Dr. Phipps of the VA Hospital was a board certified clinical psychiatrist. After a lengthy interview, he told Wells that Ted was a good candidate for a program the he was heading up. When Wells asked the success rate of this hallucinogenic therapy, Dr. Phipps apologized.

"I'm sorry Mr. Wells, but those results are classified but I have to tell you this, we are ready to begin the nineteen fifties with new, modern treatment and I'm excited. We're not in the dark ages anymore."

Wells thanked him for his trouble and said his goodbyes.

Dr. Stoeller, from Baltimore, had a more reasonable approach. He told Wells that all patients were examined and evaluated before any recommendations or prognoses were to be offered.

Wells inquired," Have you ever prescribed hallucinogenic therapy?"

"No, and I never will," he snapped back. "I don't play God with my patients." He continued giving Wells a background and description of the drug and its results. Then he told Wells, that he primarily used electro-shock treatments and that he would be happy to forward an application.

Wells drank a lukewarm cup of tea as he stared down at the town from his study window. Low clouds drifted through the quiet town, giving it a mystical, dreamy affect. He simply wanted to make a difference, for Carol's sake. Their options were few.

Wells noticed the faded green Ford pickup again.

Probably day workers, he thought.

FINAL PREP

Artie's trips to Wells' neighborhood had become frequent and, until this morning, he thought no one would notice him. This morning, Wells walked to the window and looked right at him. Artie froze until Wells walked away from the window, then he drifted the truck down the hill without the engine running. At the bottom of the hill, he put the truck in gear, turned the key and drove toward home. He cursed himself for being so sloppy.

His original plan was to watch the house and get into their daily routine. When he discovered the weak spot in their routine, he would grab the kid. There was just one problem; there was no routine. The little girl came and went at all hours of the day and night and it seemed for just about any reason under the sun.

After the events of this day, Artie had a new agenda. Pick the day, watch, follow, stay ready, then pounce when the opportunity was ripe.

Mark had always taken orders from Artie. No matter how embarrassing, degrading, menial or hard, Mark always did what he was told. Now Artie had to prep Mark for the kidnapping. Mark listened intently during each planning session and, he became more unsettled at each one. The day after Artie was nearly spotted at Wells' home, Mark made the mistake of asking one simple question about provisions. Artie went into such a tirade about who was smart enough to be in charge and who was the real leader that when he had finished Mark felt ashamed and embarrassed. He had no more questions.

AND JUST IN CASE YOU FORGOT . . .

Carol questioned Wells daily regarding the status of the tree.

"Which day will the tree come?" she asked.

"Probably, on Saturday."

"Why, just probably? Aren't you sure?"

"Yes, I'm sure."

"How's come it can't come quicker?"

"I don't know, I'll ask the foreman."

"Do you want me to ask?"

"No thanks, I'll do it."

"OK. Don't forget."

"Goodbye, Carol."

"I sent my letter to ol' Santy Claus. I told him to bring my stuff here."

"That's fine Carol."

"I was gonna give the letter to you to give him down to the TV station but Aunt Doreen says it gotta go to the North Pole. Is that right?"

"Your Aunt is a wise lady Carol."

"You know people look different on TV?"

"On TV, Santy Claus looks kinda saggy and his beard looks loose. You ever notice that?"

"No."

"Well ok, bye."

"Goodbye."

Carol exited the room, glancing over her shoulder with a stern look to give Wells the full impact of the meeting. It was just twelve days until Christmas. A trip was planned to Beckley and Carol checked on the status of that project each day as well. The child knew instinctively the significance of the holiday. She worked at it as hard as any essential piece of life.

Wells whispered, "That kid's taking years off my life."

He picked up the telephone and dialed the number of the television station.

'BOUT TIME

Wells was becoming more visible these days. On the pretense of household business, he would drift into the kitchen almost every other day. His inquiry always ended with a cup of coffee and a snack of some sort.

"I think he's just a little lonely's all," Helen said.

"He's Christmas snoopin.' I can see it in his eyes," Doreen countered.

A few mornings later, Wells sat in the kitchen opposite Carol. Wells was reading the Editorial page in the Charleston Gazette with an expression that changed from frown to sneer with each line read. An opposing political machine was taking cheap shots at a fellow citizen of the county, the governor.

Carol, on the other hand, was helping her aunt. Doreen had just mixed up a chocolate cake from scratch and Carol was wiping the mixing bowl with her finger and in turn licking the finger clean. The angel halo listed precariously to the left side of her head. This caught Wells' eye.

"Carol, may I ask you a question?" he began.

The little arm slowly circled the bowl and pulled it in tighter. "What?"

"Well, you seem to be wearing your angel costume a lot. Are you practicing for the Christmas pageant today?" he asked.

"No," she answered in a matter-of-fact tone.

He waited. Finally he asked, "Well, then, why are you always wearing your halo?"

"Cause Aunt Doreen says the picture on the television comes in better when I got it on."

Wells drifted into deep thought on the subject of the coat

hanger and aluminum foil and the television.

Carol finished cleaning the bowl and suddenly turned and said, "Hey Mr. Wells, I know what we ain't got.

"You shouldn't use the word, ain't."

"Why not."

"It is not a proper word."

"It ain't?"

"No, It is not." *Time to move on*, he thought. "What is it that we don't have?" he added.

"We don't gotta tree stand thing," she said with a knowing nod.

"We always nail a few boards across the bottom of the tree," he replied.

The woman on the television says ya' gotta get a tree stand thing or the house'll burn down!" she argued.

"The boards will work just fine."

"Them boards ain't no damn good!"

"You shouldn't say damn."

Her eyes narrowed and the brows raised, "Well then, why did you say it."

"To point out to you how wrong it is," he replied calmly.

"Well then, point it out to yourself," she snapped.

"Why are you so dedicated to the decorating of the tree and the house, Carol?" he countered.

"Cause if we don't get this place whipped into shape, ol' Santy Claus ain't gonna think it's fit to bring presents to! What in the world is wrong with you, don't you know nothin'?"

"Then, of course, by all means, you must get Doreen and drive to a store and buy one of these tree stands, while I just go and . . . and . . . rest!" he growled.

"OK!"

"Goodbye!"

After, what seemed an eternity of moments, the Chevy rolled down the drive, onto the street, and then left toward town.

"Sharp-tongued little heathen," Wells whispered to himself.

Just on a whim, Doreen thought they might find a tree stand at the Power Company's store. The clerk told Doreen he didn't carry the stands, but he informed her that the Southern States Co-operative had a few Christmas items and also the Sears and Roebucks Catalog shop across from the Courthouse had a few things on a display as well.

Doreen heard a bell beside her and looked down. Carol handed her a sleigh-bell door chime and said, "Get this."

Carol glanced around while Doreen paid the clerk. When the chime was being put into a bag, Carol yelled, "I'll wait for ya' in the car!" Then she was out the door and into the Chevy.

As Doreen started down the few steps to the sidewalk, she glanced at the impatient imp in her front seat. Carol returned the look casually, then suddenly bolted onto her knees, pointed at Doreen and yelled, silently behind the Chevy's glass.

Doreen's head jolted forward.

Doreen's world became quiet, as though listening to a seashell . . . a soft, hushed roar. She fell to her knees. She fought to keep her balance. She fought to keep her consciousness.

For a moment the, the volume came back up. The reality of the moment opened only to be stunned by the pain in her head. She fought to stand. She reached for the screaming child.

The coal miner slugged her in the back of the head again. This time she dropped.

When Artie stepped over Doreen, he reached down, took the keys from her fingers. As he opened the door, Carol started to get out the other side. He quickly reached across, grabbed the braided hair and gave a sharp yank. As the child started to fight, she started to give him her ‘what for’ speech, punctuated with a few special words she’d picked up from her Aunt Doreen. As he pulled the shifter into low and let out on the clutch, he delivered a slap to the side of Carol’s face that left her ear ringing and cheek numb for several minutes.

The Chevy rolled down Hill Street, then to Lincoln Ave., then onto Chambers Pond Road.

With glistening eyes, Carol lifted her head and glared at her captor again. At the moment of eye contact, Artie slapped her again, this time on top the head. Moments later the car stopped. Carol was lifted roughly off the seat and carried down a tight path, often going head first through thistle and greenbrier.

At the paths end stood a huge, awkward-looking man beside a truck. The big man looked as frightened as Carol felt.

Artie handed Carol off to Mark. “Keep her down and quiet,” he snapped.

Mark held Carol out before him clumsily, like a child picking up a puppy. Suddenly the puppy kicked Mark squarely in the groin. He froze.

“Didn’t do it right,” Carol thought, *“Better do it again.”* The little foot shot out and connected.

Mark extended his now weakening arms. He stumbled toward the truck as his cousin laughed.

“You dumb ass,” said Artie.

“But Artie, she’s such a little thing,” choked Mark as he placed her on the seat between them.

“Don’t say my name again, asshole!” screamed Artie.

The truck rolled alone down the dirt road unnoticed. It was an invisible entity. The sawdust tires seemed to only whisper as they pulled onto the blacktop and picked up speed. When a car approached, as rehearsed, Mark shielded the little head beside him from view. All the while, Carol studied her captors, especially the giant. When he returned her look, by instinct, the little chin shot out in defiance. She immediately expected to be slapped again. Instead, the giant quickly looked away.

Night started to fall.

AND DOREEN...

When Doreen went down with the second punch, she hit the side of her head on the curb.

She was out about a minute. Then, again, she tried to bolt upright, only to drop to one elbow. She sat still, dazed. Blood trickled from her mouth and the back of her head started to swell.

Little by little her senses came back. She realized who she was, then where she was. Then she realized Carol was gone. Her sobs were like spasms. Her rationale left.

The pain came in searing throbs of blinding light. "Why won't somebody help me?" Doreen cried, choking on her tears.

Coy was on his way to Prince's Store. He was off duty and was headed there for his usual odds, ends, and conversation.

The Mercury cut the corner wide, onto Main and headed down toward Hill St. He looked over to admire a fairly new DeSoto. As he passed the car, he saw a body on the curb. With his second look, he realized it was Doreen. He saw the blood.

The Mercury slid sideways in the street and the driver's door flew open. With three steps, he was kneeling at her side.

Coy cradled her head as he folded his jacket into a pillow. She fought. She shielded her eyes and wailed low.

"You're the cop?" She whispered.
"Yeah"
"He took little Carol," she cried in a sobbing vibrato.

"Who did!" Coy asked, his blood rapidly icing over.

"The one 'at hit me."

"What color was his hair? Was he tall?"

"No, shorter—why you askin' this?" Suddenly, Doreen cried out and held her hands over her eyes. Coy looked behind at the storefront. When he saw no one in sight, he reached below the curb, grabbed a handful of loose gravel and pelted the picture window as hard as he could.

He returned his attention to Doreen. "What was he driving?"

"My car," she whispered.

The door of the Power Company store jerked open, "What the hell's a goin' on out here!"

"Call the Sheriff and the doctor, now," Coy shouted.

Bob Kennedy looked down at Coy on the sidewalk, " I don't know what the hell's a goin' on down there, but . . ."

"GET HELP! CALL THE SHERIFF NOW YOU STUPID SON OF A BITCH!"

The clerk ran for the telephone.

"What was he wearing?" Coy watched her eyes wander, trying to focus.

"Work clothes. Why'd he hit me?"

Doreen fought the darkness, only to find delirium. Lights spun around her. She reached out. Only glimpses. The tall old cop, Doc' Stark, Wells, Helen. She tried to catch sight of Carol.

Nothing.

Darkness.

TO THE HIDEOUT

State route 52 follows the Gauley River through town. Then after almost four miles, the road crosses the railroad tracks and starts up a steep grade. Two miles from those tracks, that old green Ford pickup made a complete u-turn onto an old overgrown rock based, abandoned strip-mine road. The grade was so steep, the Ford's gear shift remained in low for the climb.

When the truck reached the summit, Artie threw the shifter down and let the truck race sure-footed, along a road that was now just two paths in the broom sage.

The truck slowed a bit as it passed through a high heavy gate and fence.

Beside the gate stood a tall watchtower. It had been erected during a wildcat strike in 1942. Since all coal was crucial to the war effort, the federal government and state militia showed no sympathy to striking miners. Any mine affected by a strike was immediately converted into a fortress. The mines were fenced in and sentries policed the area. In the towers at the gates, guards armed with machine guns routed all picketers.

A few men died and for patriotic reasons, the strike waned.

Artie had stocked the abandoned mine superintendent's office with all necessities: food, drink, and bedding. The windows were boarded up, so keeping the brat inside was not going to be a problem.

Two kerosene lamps were lit. One burned bright, the other strobed, dim and smoky. Artie lit his Camel with the same match. He blew the smoke through a satisfied grin. *So far, so good*, he thought.

Mark was still following his orders in perfect sequence. He led Carol to the table, cautiously then sat opposite her at the table. Mark then reached into a cooler and a box of supplies, serving her cereal and milk. She just sat. He then poured himself a bowl and started to eat. Slowly, Carol joined in the meal, never looking up.

Artie entered from the back door. "OK, cousin, you know the routine, next she sleeps, in there. And lock the damn door and don't let her kick ya' in the gonads no more! Ha ha ha." The laughter ended when the truck started.

Mark stared after him, disappointed and embarrassed. Then, he turned his eyes to Carol. She returned the stare, coldly. His eyes quickly dropped to the cereal bowl.

"Why do you hate me?" came the sharp little voice.
"I—I d don't ha . . . hate you," was all he could say.

He led her to her bed. Mark left a small candle on a crate away from her bedding. He just pointed at the bedding, walked out, and latched the door.

Mark sat by the table and stared at the door.

Mark heard Carol moving about in the makeshift bedroom. He tried to guess with each sound, what the child was doing. It grew quiet. Mark moved closer and peered through the keyhole. In the shadows of the flickering candle, the only thing Mark could see were two small hands held tightly together atop the wool blanket.

The child took a deep breath and began.

"Well . . . God, it's me again. I ain't sure what's a goin' on down here. I sure hope my Aunt Doreen is okay. I hope my Mom ain't too scared, and . . . um I'm tryin' not to get scared either, but it's hard. If you see my mom or my daddy or Mr. Wells, you might tell 'em where I am and that I'm okay. Well, I let you go now so's you can go check on my Aunt Doreen on account o' that son of o' . . . well, never mind. Boy, this is hard God. Amen an' good night."

Mark backed away from the door, staring at the keyhole. He lowered his head.

AN' THEN...

Coy gave a brief report to Wells and Helen as they stood in the hallway outside the emergency room of Oak Hill Memorial Hospital. When he had shared all that he knew to date, he began questioning them.

"Has anyone seemed suspicious to ya lately?"

"No, not really," answered Wells uneasily.

Coy waited for Helen's nod to make it unanimous.

He then looked at Wells and asked, "Are you the little girl's daddy?"

"Of course not," snapped Wells. The shock on his face was proof enough.

Helen answered softly, "Carol's daddy is in the VA Hospital down in Beckley. He's got a psychological problem from the war. I just work for Mr. Wells, with my Aunt Doreen there." She said pointing to her aunt as she lay on the bed. "Me an' Carol live over the garage at Mr. Wells' home."

"I'll be damned," Coy replied.

"What?" barked Wells.

"Oh, nothing," said Coy, "Gotta go. I'll check with ya after while. Thanks."

Wells followed the old trooper outside. "Officer Browning."

"Sir?"

"Spare nothing. Do you understand."

"Yeah, I think I know what you mean and that's kinda how I operate anyhow."

Coy went to his car, his mind racing. He always lit his cigarette with a safety match. The spent match went out the window as the car went into second gear. His mind outran the car. "First thing to do is check the obvious," he mused as he pulled into the station house. When he reached the jail, he phoned the State Police barracks in Beckley. Coy explained the situation and they agreed to go to the hospital and check on the girl's father.

This could be just a plain old kidnapping. Hell, he even thought Wells was related to the girl. If the kidnappers thought the same thing then time would become an enemy. The kidnappers might do anything if they realized their mistake.

Two hours later Coy called the hospital and asked for Wells.

"Wells here."

"How's Miss McIlhenney doin'?"

"She's about the same, thank you."

Coy then explained his concern about a possible kidnapping.

"I'll have to say, I agree in principle," Wells replied.

Coy continued, "Better to be careful and say nothing. We have ta keep this as quiet as possible. You might explain it to the girl's mama too." He then signed off.

Coy had been on cases like this before. He thought the day through again, went to a jail cell, dropped the cot and laid down. He forced himself to sleep. *Tomorrow morning will be rough.*

Emerson Holiday walked in. "Coy, you seem to have taken full charge here and to be honest, I'm kinda glad you did. You got more trainin' at this than the rest of us, but you act like you got a personal interest in this thing."

Coy took the last drag on the Pall Mall and said, "She's a friend."

"What time you want up?"

"When the phone rings."

The state trooper walked into the Veterans Hospital on the edge of Beckley at 12:45am. He searched for someone to inquire of the whereabouts of one Ted McMurfree.

He stood and listened to a distant noise. He started in that direction.

He passed an open door and glanced in.

“Where do you think you’re going, buster?” came a voice from inside.

Trooper Maynard Lance stepped back and centered in the door and came face to face with the one and only Nurse Yolonda Mae Yochlotski.

“Yes ma’am, I need to verify the whereabouts of one Ted McMurfree.”

“Well, son, you come to the right place and probably to the right person but we’re just gonna have to see just who you are before we proceed. Do you understand, son?”

“Yes ma’am, I understand completely.”

“So how we gonna establish this, huh?

“Listen carefully, I’m assisting in a very recent crime investigation. This can be very easy or I can go over your head. It makes no matter to me, lady,” said the trooper through clenched teeth.

She started to protest when she was interrupted by her supervisor.

“Hello, I’m Nurse Davis, the evening supervisor. You may go back to your duties Miss Yochlotski. Find something to mop. Now how may I help you officer?” she asked as she watched her subordinate retreat. Moments later, the trooper followed Nurse Davis as she unlocked and relocked their way deeper into the institution.

Upon entering Ted’s ward, Nurse Davis asked what was the crime.

“A child is missing.”

“Well, they’ll normally turn up, you know. Whose kid was it?”

“This McMurfree guy’s kid, the way I understand it.”

Nurse Davis rolled Ted over a bit to show the trooper his face.

"This is him. Why do you want to see him?" she asked.

"I guess to make sure he didn't kidnap his own kid."

"Well it wasn't him."

After they left, Ted lay there confused. *Someone took Carol. Someone took Carol. Why?*

Ted dropped to the floor and crawled to the door and listened and watched their feet as they walked down the long hall. Nurse Davis was muttering an apology and asking more of the kidnapping.

" . . .and I reckon when they took the kid they beat the hell outta some woman. Then they drove off in her own car. "

"What in the devil do you suppose this worlds comin' to?" the nurse inquired.

"Hey, you're 'bout the classiest woman I ever met. What're ya' doin' Saturday night?"

The trooper and the nurse walked through the door at the hall's end.

A CAGE OPEN

Ted walked over and dressed quickly then walked back and squatted by the door. He closed his eyes trying to adjust to the night. When his eyes reopened —a fierce, wild-eyed glare had settled into them.

Ted took the pin of his belt buckle, held it under the hinge pin and drove it out with the heel of his shoe. After all three hinge pins were clear, Ted took the buckle pin and pried the hinge out and grabbed it with his fingers. Within moments the door cracked and sprung to one side.

Ted covered the length of the hallway quickly. One fire escape door was usually left unlocked so the employees could access the cafeteria next door. Everyone including Ted knew of the door. The night air was cool and Ted moved quickly to keep warm. He was about a mile from Route 19, the road to Oak Hill. He covered the rough terrain in minutes, then squatted in the brush deciding what to do next.

Before his Army days, Ted was a high-spirited, methodical lad. His father was forty-eight when Ted was born and was a good father until his death when Ted was ten. Because his mentor was old, Ted always rationalized his problems like an old man. The Army changed all of that. His problem solving skills now consisted of two things, objective and solution. He decided his first objective would be to get to Oak Hill.

The emotionally ill soldier ran head long into the night.

THE POSSE FORMS

Coy bolted upright in the jail bunk. "How long have you been there?"

"Just moments actually," answered Wells, sitting in a chair beside the cot.

"Sneakin' up on a fellar is a habit I could break you of," said Coy. He lit the match and the tip of the Pall Mall turned a cherry red as he took the first drag. In the dim lighting, Wells' eyes reflected the red glow of the cigarette eerily back toward the trooper.

"Sorry," said Wells, "I've been thinking about things at my disposal that could be of assistance.

"Like what?"

"I have horses, jeeps, an airplane and even a helicopter is at my disposal. One of my contemporaries in Elkins has one. He said I could have it for the duration. The Governor is a friend and would help out, I'm sure."

"Listen Wells, all the kings horses and all the kings helicopters ain't gonna help if they don't know where to look, and this country is big."

Deputy sheriff Holiday hollered back to Coy. "Hey big guy, are you up?"

"Yeah I'm up, Doc."

"You want some o' this coffee then."

Coy flipped the eye of the pocket watch over. 5:20. "Yeah."

"Then I s'pose you'll be wantin' your messages?" inquired the deputy.

"What messages?"

"Oh, this come a little bit ago."

Holiday gave Coy the coffee and the note as Coy pulled the light switch. His eyes adjusted to the light as they raced back and forth across the page.

"Damn," he whispered.

"What is it?" asked Wells.

Coy led him back to the end of the hall. Coy began speaking quietly. "It looks like whoever done this thought the girl belongs to you."

"That's silly. I ..."

Coy held up his hand in an effort to halt the sentence. "No, it ain't silly. Hell, I thought it myself when I met her at old Prince's store."

Wells mind raced. "What do you suggest?"

"Go home and answer the phone. Play along with it. We'll take the next step when it's handed to us."

"Is there anything else that I can do?" Wells asked.

"No but listen. I'm going by the hospital to see if Doreen is conscious. I need to ask her more questions, then I'll be over. If they call, stall 'em for as long as you can. See if you can make 'em get Carol talk to you on the phone. That'll make 'em bring her out of hiding."

"What was the message from the deputy?"

"I checked to see if Carol's dad was missing. Thought maybe he might have something in on this, but he was still in his bed."

Wells seemed somewhat relieved, "That's a blessing."

"What do you mean?"

"Oh nothing, I'll tell you when you get to the house."

"Okay, go then."

Wells walked to the Cadillac, turned the key and roared across the tracks and up the hill.

Coy grabbed a towel and headed for the shower.

Holiday yelled again. "Hey Coy, you want some breakfast?"

"Ain't got time."

"Just thought I'd be neighborly."

The cold water opened his eyes.

Coy walked into ward #3 at 6:35 am. Doreen's bed was at the other end of the ten-bed ward. No other patients were here. A doctor, a nurse and Helen were standing by the bed.

Helen saw him approach and looked for some sign in his face. The hope in her eyes waned and she turned her gaze back to Doreen.

"Any change?" Coy asked, softly.

"None." Helen's voice was a whisper.

"Has she said anything or mumbled anything through the night?" Coy continued.

"She's mumbled but nothing you could understand," answered the nurse.

Coy felt helpless then said, "I gotta go. When she says anything, call me."

Coy noticed the phone on the nightstand as he spoke, "Is that a private line?"

"Yes, do you need the number?" asked the nurse.

"Yes." Coy replied.

Helen couldn't look up when he left.

FORCE MARCH

Ted watched the trucks approach and crouched even lower in the brush. He had thought he could hitch a ride to Oak Hill, but the thought of approaching another man was overwhelming. After what seemed like an eternity. He stood and waited and then paced.

When he saw no traffic he ran. The only thing he could think to do was run. When a car or truck came along Ted would dive over the bank or lay in the tall brush. The going was slow but he had no choice. He would run and run wildly. When he was winded, he'd lay covered in sweat in the undergrowth just below the roadway. After resting, the cycle would repeat, and repeat, for hours.

Ted saw the glow of lights ahead. The town of Jazbo was still alive at 3:10 AM. The town consisted of a tidy and proud Main Street, an intersection of a town square with small nicely constructed businesses and homes, and successive rings of houses, shacks, and buildings of lesser and lesser value, a well laid out boomtown. Ted belly crawled past the lighted areas. On the edge of the town he was jumping from bush to bush when a German police dog came from nowhere. Ted's reaction was swift. He stunned the animal with a quick heel chop to the forehead, then with its own chain, tied up its mouth and legs like a calf at the rodeo. The pile of dog and steel chain lay still, apart from the animal whimpering softly as Ted patted its chest and whispered an apology.

As he started up the mountain out of Jazbo, traffic picked up. Ted started his run again. A coal truck approached and he scrambled down the bank only to find a rain culvert about five feet in height. He sat and rested. Then his head dropped and he slept.

Although not a record, Ted had traveled 13 miles in 8 hours. He'd once carried a friend fifteen miles in hostile territory in Korea. The remainder of the platoon had died in battle. Ted had searched for survivors to save lives or maybe not to be alone. One man clung to life and he carried him out.

Other faces, dead and mutilated, still haunted him. In a rapidly progressing withdrawal from his heavy doses of medication, the young veteran contended with many evils in the ever-dissolving views in the night.

...AND THE REST

Artie had spent the evening first in the Lone Horse Tavern then asleep in his truck outside. He was known to do this from time to time and he felt it secured his alibi. When he awoke, he drove through town just to see what activity he could spot. Nothing stirred at this early hour and he headed out of town. When he reached home, he bathed, had a shot and a beer to quiet the throbbing in his head, and smiled as though he hadn't a care in the world. Artie finished a breakfast of fried eggs and baloney from the old black skillet, then settled in for a late morning nap.

Mark stared at the door.

"I've got a little problem, mister?" came the little girl's voice.

"Uh, . . . What?"

"I've really got to use the bathroom," answered Carol.

Mark had been trained for this dilemma. The door opened to find the munchkin rocking back and forth, from one foot to the other, arms folded.

Mark took her hand and led her to the outhouse next to the office.

She spoke loudly so he could hear her through the outhouse door.

"I'm really getting used to that city livin' buddy. An' I'm really used to inside bathrooms. This thing is cold!" The door swung open. "OK. All done."

He held out the hand. They walked back into the old office.

Mark stared at her as if she were a doll or a manikin in Lear's display window.

"Hey, don't you think it's about time for breakfast" she barked.

He smiled and nodded his head. He took her hand and she led him into the abandoned office for breakfast.

THE LAWYER'S MISTRESS

Marguerite walked over and tapped lightly on the Florentine patterned glass of McKinney's inner office door. There was no answer. She tapped louder.

"Yes, what do you want," came the sleepy voice.

Marguerite stuck her head through the door, "Peter, I just came back from the Post Office and someone had slipped this envelope under the door."

"What is it?"

"Well, I didn't open it," she said, holding out the manila envelope close enough for him to read. It said, 'Strictly Confidential - T.G. Wells only'.

McKinney snapped to attention, "I'll handle this, thanks."

"And Pete, honey…."

"What?"

"Comb your hair, darling," she giggled and strutted toward her desk away from her freshly seduced quarry.

Peter called Wells immediately wanting to know if any correspondence was to be expected. At first Wells seemed put off by his call, but then McKinney told him what it was. Within seconds Peter was running toward his car, hair uncombed and puzzled at why the old man had gone so berserk.

Ten minutes later, Coy held the paper up to a light to look for smudges and prints.

"What is it?" inquired old Wells.

"Just looking."

Coy turned the note over. He studied it a bit then flipped it over again and stared at the cut out letters and words.

'We have the girl - she will die unless you pay. Will call later.'

Coy stared into the foyer at McKinney.

"Better get rid of him and tell him to keep his mouth shut. We don't need any kind o' trouble now."

Wells marched the length of the living room and into the foyer. "Peter, you better go back now. And, oh, by the way if any of this gets out, there will be hell to pay and I do mean hell." Well's hard stare followed his words of warning.

As he ended the pep talk, the heel of the automatic pistol came into view, tucked into the belt of his trousers.

Peter McKinney shuddered at the sight of the gun.

"It hadn't taken much skin for the lawyer to get charges dismissed against Wells for wounding a strike-breaker from the Coal Operators Association who had attacked one of his men. Strikebreakers had been hired to randomly attack picketers and generally break the spirit of those on strike. When Wells pulled into the entrance of his Rosella No. 2 Mine, two strikebreakers had a lone picketer on the ground and were kicking him in the head and abdomen.

Wells had deftly handled the situation with no remorse whatsoever. During the trial he turned to look at the jury and simply stated, "If my men go on strike, it's between me and them and no one else."

"Now Peter, just go back to your office and wait for my call. Or if you hear anything, you call me. Understand?"

"Yes, sir," he offered weakly.

"And Peter, if any one asks and I mean anyone, the child who lives here is mine." Wells put one hand on his hip and rested the other on the butt of the pistol. "Are you sure you understand . . . completely?"

Peter knew the old man very well. Wells never took any situation lightly that could be taken hard.

"Yes, I understand completely," said Peter.

As McKinney entered his office he glanced at Marguerite.

"Cancel everything!"

"Why?" she said.

He looked over and rolled his eyes and held up his hands. "Just do it!" His door slammed, rattling the small panes of glass.

ALONE

Not a soul heard the growls and cries coming from the storm culvert on the edge of the blacktop roadway on the southern side of Wiley's Ridge. Ted had awakened at 9:AM with cramps in both legs. He just wasn't used to the walking. The night before he had walked and then ran in a continuing cycle to keep his mind occupied. Now, as he stirred and tried to move about to loosen up, the demons of drug withdrawal were closing in on him again. He prayed for Nurse Davis to strut in and calm him with a dose of that 'old VA magic', a pet name for the psyche medication given by one of the patients there.

The culvert was a cage for the animal he'd become. Every time he tried to crawl out and up onto the road, a vehicle would come into sight and the internal rage would return the timid veteran to his culvert.

Ted now rocked on his heels, squatting and growling through clenched teeth, his voice drowned out by a rumbling below. He leaned out of the culvert and looked down. An empty coal train rolled by, heading for Oak Hill.

The train crested the ridge and started down the grade. After the long line of soot-covered coal cars passed, the bright red caboose finished the train. Ted envisioned a red fox jumping from tree to tree in rapid succession, giving chase to a shadow. Then it was gone. The lone traveler found a lonelier trail to follow - the rails. Ted slid down the steep embankment and stepped on to the rail ties.

After a walking several hours, he came to an intersection in the tracks. He stood still facing a crossroads that could take him either toward home or into what felt at this moment to be an abyss. Ted felt frozen in a moment filled with fear, guilt, and the cringe of drug withdrawal, and after a time, he tried one direction for several yards, then the other. He was standing with clenched fists when he saw the sign forty yards ahead on the right track. When he reached the sign and read it, his body formed a posture of hopelessness. His head and shoulders drooped. He hugged his chest as though pulling into himself.

The sign noted the direction of the next town – 'Mount

Hope'. The problem was they had abbreviated the name to 'Mt Hope', only Ted read it in its most basic form, M T Hope - he saw it as 'empty hope'.

Ted started to walk away in this same posture but only made it twenty feet. He walked back and looked at the sign again. *Empty hope.* With forlorn and downcast eyes, he looked around as though he were being watched, then at the sign again. He walked thirty feet from the sign this time, then turned and stared. He read it again.

If there was one thing he was an expert of, Ted knew the people of these hills. He knew that they were of the best and worst the world had to offer. He knew that one of them had his daughter. His arms dropped from his chest and his hands and fingers formed into angry claws. A raw power reverberated from his hands, up through his arms and met in the center of his spine and then on. Ted lowered his head and with this renewed primal strength he walked toward the marker. As he stood before the sign and read '*Empty hope*' for the last time, he emitted a low growl.

In the following spring, a maintenance crew from C&O Railroad made their way to repair the sign at Mount Hope junction. As they replaced the mangled piece of steel, they debated as to whether the sign was destroyed by a wild animal or perhaps a piece of equipment that had fallen from a train and hit the sign. Several scenarios of the sign's destruction were suggested, but none really fit. It never occurred to them that a tall scrawny boy from Otter Hollow could have done this. There simply wasn't much left to repair.

THE KIDS

"I really, really, really, really, really fink that you should take me to Mr. Wells house right now!" demanded Carol. The arms were crossed and the lip was out and the eyes were narrowed.

Big Mark just cowered. "I can't and, and, and! I'm really… really sorry, OK"

"I did five 'reallys' and you only did two," she said.

"Huh?"

"I am going home right now!"

"I don't think you can walk that far, ya see we're way out here and I don't think I could even walk that far," Mark stated beneath furrowed pleading brows.

Carol understood that Mark was almost the same age as she was, but she didn't understand why he was so big and so old looking. He was like some of the people at her Dad's hospital. Mark was happy to finally be in the company of a person who let him express himself, completely.

Mark pulled out his pocket watch and studied it carefully. "In a little bit more it will be time for lunch."

"What do we have to eat," asked Carol, suddenly putting on airs.

"We got some baloney, some bread, an' mustard and' some coke and it ain't too cold so ya gotta be careful 'bout it foamin' up in your nose."

"Let's not have lunch," said Carol. Mark waited, wide eyed.

"Let's have a tea party."

"But it's coke," said Mark.

"But we will pretend it's tea."

"Oh, okay, I reckon, but I never been to a tea party."

"Me neither."

"I been to a pancake feed," said Mark.

"No, we're not having a pancake feed," snapped Carol.

"Been to a bean dinner."

"No thank you," said Carol.

"How's about a ramp dinner?" asked Mark.

"What's a ramp?"

"It's kinda like a onion…'ceptin' more stronger."

"Couldn't stand the smell…you ain't payin' attention, now listen to me, TEA PARTY, OK?!"

"Oh, okay, but why a tea party?" he said.

"Well, on account of I asked Santy Claus for a tea set for Christmas."

"You ever been to a tea party?" asked the giant.

"No, but Aunt Doreen says it's what uppity people do on Tuesday mornins'," she replied.

"You're not uppity Carol."

"I might be when I grow up so I guess I might as well give it a whirl."

"OK. We'll do the tea party," he replied.

"Then, after the tea party I'm a goin' home to Mr. Wells' house on account a Christmas is purty damn soon an' if ol' Santy Claus can't find me there ta' give me my damn presents, why how else will I get'em. An' you know what else, it'll be your fault, it'll be on your head! Mind what I'm tellin' you, boy!" she barked while wagging the tiny finger.

Mark held his hand up to try to fend off Carol's words as though they were a curse.

"I can't let you go. Artie would hit me. Please Carol? Don't get me in trouble…OK?"

The responsibilities were becoming too much!

ALONE

Helen decided to use the shower at the hospital to freshen up. She pulled the curtain and listened to the water drum the porcelain-covered steel. When it had warmed she stepped inside and rested her head against the wall as the hot water hit her back. The cadence of the water beating the shower walls seemed to quicken her thoughts into a feeling of urgency. Doreen hadn't stirred. Wells was gone. Helen was alone with her thoughts and fears. She imagined the best outcome and then she imagined the worst.

The water relaxed her and the steam seemed to help soften her eyes. She choked on her own sobs, but only for a moment. There wasn't time for this nonsense. But was it all nonsense. This night she felt alone, completely and utterly and devastatingly alone. Neither Helen's fears nor her anger could replace what was gone. Her heart only seemed to be beating on one side.

Helen quickly washed, then as she rinsed off, suddenly, she froze. Helen lowered to her knees and looking upward as though seeking peace in a driving storm, she closed her eyes and put her palms together.

..WELL, IT JUST KEEPS ON GETTING THICKER

Peter McKinney was relaxing now. He had rationalized that the matters at hand weren't his fault. He was simply being used as an instrument in this awful ordeal. The gin also was helpful in this rationalization. The phone rang once. Marguerite answered in the outer office, but didn't use the intercom. "Probably just a normal call," mumbled the lawyer.

She tapped the door twice. "Peter?" she inquired.

"Come in."

Margaret stepped through the door and stopped. "A man called and said to tell them to be in the downtown office at 6 tonight, then he just hung up. What's it mean?"

"Nothing," he replied, bluntly.

"It sure is strange in here today."

Pete pulled on his jacket and ran through the door without answering.

"What do ya want me to do!"

"Stay here!"

She watched him race his car up the hill toward the old man's house. She smiled as she lit the cigarette in her teeth. *Like shootin' fish.*

THEY DEW DROP, DON'T THEY…

Artie had gone through the curtain and back the narrow hall toward the bathrooms. Frank had converted his dead Uncle Lando's house into the "Daily Dew Drop Inn" and in retrospect considered the large foyer an added classy touch to his 'not so classy' bar. Within the large entrance, he was able to frame in two small bathrooms, add a bench and large coat rack, and it was a good place to put the pay phone.

Artie started drinking Black Labels at 1:30 and his trips to the bathroom and to the phone to call to Marguerite, went unnoticed. She had rehearsed her lines to perfection. She needed no prompting. Artie made sure no one else was listening and had simply stated, "Don't screw it up!"

When Artie returned from the phone, Frank was in a heated discussion with Mitch Blakesmith over stolen pickled eggs and beets.

"I never stole no damn eggs nor no damn beets neither, an' I don't appreciate being called no damn egg thief neither!" he slurred. "Besides, you was out in the back room an' I don't remember you leavin' one o' your damn eyes here on the bar while you was gone."

"You took 'em an' by damn you'll pay fer 'em!" barked the bartender.

The bartender started to roll up his sleeves. Sensing eminent defeat, the egg thief conceded as gracefully as any drunk could, besides, he remembered just a few years back when Frank had boxed semi-professionally up at Wheeling and had even whipped the boxing bear at the Braxton County fair, two years in a row.

"I'd like to propose a toast to the smartest man in this here beer garden! Why ol' Frank here is another one o' them Sherluck Holmes kinda fellers. I don't know how ya' figured it out, ol' buddy, but I propose a toast to ya' any ol' damn way." The drunk raised the glass with his purple arm and said, "Here's to ol' Frank, by damn!"

After another beer, Artie started complaining and just giving "ole Frank" a rough time about being a cheap skate. Frank wasn't in the mood.

Artie bought the next round of beer at the A&P store on the corner of Main and Jefferson. He also picked up some bread and baloney. *Mark probably ate that whole box of food by now,* he thought.

Artie started the truck, opened a warm beer, and headed for Marguerite's father's house to make the ransom call to Wells. Marguerite had set the phone on her dad's porch that morning. Artie feared old Ed Reed would hear the phone and carry it back inside, but after 40 years of running his loader at the main line tipple, he could barely hear the television when it was turned up full tilt, like it was now.

Artie sat in his truck and grabbed a new bottle. The beer relaxed him, but he still kept repeating his own rehearsed lines and practiced replies. He opened the beer on the truck's door-handle, stood up, and walked down the path toward Marguerite's daddy's back porch.

MOUNTAIN ANGELS

Leon Cox had retired when the mine closed ten years before. Most everyone else had gone except he and Mrs. Cox and Levon Watkins.

Levon was to be in a wheel chair forever. His legs had been crushed in a roof fall and when everyone else left, he stayed behind with his friend, Leon. The company houses had been abandoned and they fit their budgets just fine, besides, this was about the only place where they truly felt welcome.

Leon had come when the mines were recruiting cheap help. His kids had moved on to Michigan and Ohio, to find their fortunes, so he and his wife and Levon cared for one another as any family would. It was a mixed family though, two members being of an African descent and one coming from a lineage of Romania Jews.

So anyway, all summer long Leon walked the tracks gathering coal that had fallen off the trains and raised his garden and a few chickens. He used the old powder house as a cellar and the company store was his chicken coup. He traded ginseng and yellow root to the engineer of the Number 47 that came through toward Clay County and by November he usually had enough to winter with. Today the weather was nice and Leon was gathering some coal and just looking around mostly.

Then he saw Ted sitting on the side of a stone culvert holding his sides. Ever so carefully, Leon walked up to Ted, as though he were approaching a wild injured animal. I guess Ted had that look in his eyes. Ted turned and looked at him warily.

"Why, what's a matter there, young fella? Are ya OK?"

The old man had walked up to him so quietly, Ted was completely caught off guard. Ted was too cramped to jump up and too tired to scramble and just too terrified to utter a note.

The old colored man just laid his thick fingers gently on Ted's shoulder, "Now don't let ole Leon scare ya boy, OK?" And amazing enough Ted wasn't frightened didn't mind the warm old calloused black hand rubbing his shoulder. Leon felt the muscles in the shoulder draw tight against the small chain he felt under his shirt.

In just moments, Ted began to relax.

"Now son, are you hurting or just wore down a bit?"

Ted looked up, and his mouth opened to speak and nothing happened. *Well he was probably out of practice,* thought Leon.

The old man said, "Never you mind son." Sensing Ted's lack of ability to communicate. "Why, I can talk 'nuff for both of us. I'll be bettin' you hungry, a looking at yo' eyes and belly."

Leon dug in his coat pocket and retrieved some corn bread wrapped up in a oil stained brown paper bag. "Now go on and eat a lil' bit of that. There's some venison in there too."

Ted took the bread and took some small bites, then chewed slowly and watched Leon as he continued to speak. "Ya see boy, ole Leon here got this big belly, well it ain't huge but it stores up a plenty so's when I got to share my lunch wif a bony ass young un' such as ya' self, then it'd not be a problem, now, 'sides, I'd be proud to help ya. You want me go down to the spring and git ya some water, boy?"

Ted continued to stare as the old man rambled. Ted was someone new to talk to and it made the old man feel good to help someone in need.

Later, as Ted was sitting up and feeling much better, he started to rub his legs.

"Hey boy, is them legs a hurtin' ya." Leon handed Ted the tin cup full of water. The clear water was strong of taste but cool, and he felt better almost immediately.

"Here boy, eat 'nother piece or take it with ya. Lord know when ya gonna meet somebody nice as me agin." Leon handed Ted the corn cake as he chuckled at his modesty.

Ted ate another bite and tried to straighten his legs as he chewed. Leon knelt down before Ted and took his leg, and again, Ted let him. Leon felt the knots his muscles had become and gently began rubbing and kneading and massaging one leg, then the other.

"Now I'm used to doing this 'count my old buddy Levon. He got busted up in a cave-in years ago, we just been kinda lookin' after him. Keepin' him warm and fed and the such, and I gotta rub his ole crippled legs all over so he can stay limber enough just ta move."

In just minutes Ted was walking slowly about. Stamping one

foot, then the other. The legs felt good.

He looked at the old man. The old man looked back and smiled, proud of his work.

"Thanks," was all Ted could get out. He nodded his head and started down the tracks, grade seemed to get steep immediately.

"Well bless my ass!" Ted looked back. "Here you can talk, and let this poor ol' colored boy beat his gums up and down this track jus' a talkin' and a chidin' away. Why you turnin' out to be almost an embarrassment to me. I ought to kick yo' lil', peckerwood ass."

For the first time in two years Ted laughed out loud. He smiled so wide that it felt strangely tight against his cheeks. He waved at the old man as the ol' man's laughter sent him on his way.

Leon turned and walked back toward Hallelujah Coal Camp, coal sack in hand and continued his conversation. "Now I'm goin' back up ta Hallelujah Camp and you better git yo' narrow white ass outta here fo' I crack it wit dis sack a coal - ha, ha, ha!" said the joyful black man with the booming voice.

"When you git on round to that second bridge, why just take the left track and it'll put ya where ya needs to be, Ted."

Ted spun to the sound of his name – no one was in sight. A small cloud of fog drifted atop the stream. Ted felt the lump of bread in his pocket to make sure it hadn't been some sort of dream.

So many dreams.

A CALL

The office phone finally rang. Wells had already pulled and plugged each line at the switchboard so he could sit in his office and wait.

Wells reached across to the phone. "Hello…yes, I'm alone."

Coy nodded from across the room.

"Listen careful, you git me $250,000 cash by tomorrow or I'll break that lil' bitch's neck,…understand."

"I understand perfectly" the old man replied coolly. "I want proof that she's safe and unharmed," Wells added.

"I kinda expected some of this crap. You'll have your gawddam proof come morning, just remember, no tricks or she'll pay."

"You have my word, and sir . . ."

"Uh, yeah"

"If any unprovoked harm comes to this child…" Wells left the inferred stand.

Artie laid the phone in its cradle and smiled.

Coy sat on the chair by the window, studying the view of the gully below as he nursed the Pall Mall. He thought, *This old man seems real steady but I believe he bears watching.*

Wells seemed to be occupied as though he were calculating something.

Coy walked out to the desk and sat opposite Wells as he continued to calculate. "What is it?" Coy asked.

"I'm just trying to figure what cash is on hand, I think we're OK. I believe I have the money.

"You're OK with paying 'em what they're asking?" said Coy.

"Oh, yes, as long as the child is delivered unharmed," replied Wells

"Then what?"

"I would think after that we would get the money back" the coal baron replied, in a matter-of-fact tone.

Coy was really beginning to admire the old man, but he didn't feel secure around him. Coy smiled and said, "Seems like we got us a plan."

Wells dialed the lawyer, "Hello, is Peter in?"

"Just a moment please," replied the secretary.

"Hello, this is Peter McKinney."

"Pete, they called and I have the amount on hand. I'll be over in a minute to set it up."

Wells took a ring of keys from the desk drawer and held the door for Coy as he flipped the button on the deadbolt to lock up.

THE GET-AWAY CAVERN

Artie hung up the phone and followed the path toward his truck. That old man Wells had really pissed him off, of course the money would help him to forget this indiscretion. The truck drifted down the alley and as he neared the end, he popped the clutch and let the weight of the truck start the engine quietly. He shifted into second gear and idled left onto the street below, heading toward the old turnpike. After opening the beer on the under side of the window crank, he followed the old turnpike road past the Civil War grave markers then turned on to a service road that followed an abandoned spur of the old railroad track. The road was built as an access to a tunnel that the C&O railroad started through Clifford's Knob. They hit so many explosive methane gas pockets that the project was forgotten barely forty feet into the hill.

He drove to the long abandoned project. The tunnel's opening was now enclosed with creosoted timber framing and covered over with corrugated tin. Several warning signs hung about.

Artie leaned backed into the truck and popped open another warm beer. Afterward he looked around slowly and carefully. When he was sure there were no bums around, he walked over to the left side of the closed opening and swung a loosely nailed sheet of tin to the side and stepped into the tunnel.

When he was inside he pulled a carbide lamp from a nail overhead and within seconds the old cave was illuminated. Before Artie sat an almost new, 1951 Crown Victoria Ford, compliments of the Riffles for the low price of $200, a fifth of Virginia Gentleman, and a twenty-five caliber derringer. Artie slid behind the seat and turned the key. The battery was still well charged and the gas gauge read full. The tires all looked properly inflated. When he turned the key, the Ford came to life.

When his eyes were adjusted to the light outside again, he looked about more carefully. After he was satisfied that all was well with the Ford and that his secret was intact, he got into the old green pickup and idled down the gravel road and into the early evening.

THE PRAYER

One hand was planted on her hip. The other hand had a small index finger wagging at Mark's face.

"Listen here buster," she continued, "I'm getting a little tired and sick of staying here. I want to go home and I want to go right now!"

"Now, I can't 'cause Artie would get mad," replied Mark with his big hands raised in frustration.

"Mark! Listen, please? Ya see, Christmas is comin' real quick but I ain't ready, so I wanna go now, . . . please!" the lip shot out, the arms folded and jaw was set.

Mark couldn't take the hard stare from the little tyrant. He lowered his head and stared at the floor. "Artie will hit me if you don't be good, an' if you be good it will be over quicker, an' now I been good to you all day and we played what you wanted to play an' I didn't say nothing when you cheated at the card game." as his voice trailed off.

"I didn't cheat!" she yelled out.

" Oh, uh, so why don't you jus' go on an' go ta bed an' tomorrow it'll probably be over with.

"I can't go to bed!" she yelled.

"Why not?"

"I gotta pee!"

"Will you go to bed then?"

"Yeah, I reckon, besides, you talk too much," she added.

Five minutes later as Mark started to pull the makeshift bedroom door closed, Carol looked up and said, "I gotta get home, Mark, I really do. I got shoppin' to get done."

Mark just nodded his head in agreement and pulled the door closed. He remained there, on one knee staring at the door.

Carol walked over to the cot and sat, just on the edge, and tried to figure it all out. *Everything that had happened in the last few days was bad. These guys were doing a bad thing, Aunt Doreen was hurt bad. She might miss Christmas and this was real bad! 'Real bad,'* she thought hard. *'Hey, wait a minute, Aunt Doreen said that when things got real bad, why that's when ya' gotta go to the Penicosal!'*

Mark had put his ear to the door the previous evening to listen to a quiet, heartfelt little girl prayer that had left a wet trail on his own cheek. Mark's ear gently rested against the door, readying for Carols little prayer.

The little girl cleared her throat, grabbed the lapel of her coat with one hand, raised the other toward heaven, and in the most resonant, authoritative, and spiritual voice she could muster, she began.

"BROTHERS AND SISTERSSA, LET US BOW ah, OUR HEADS ah, IN PRAYER ah!"

Mark's eyes widened, then in obedience he lowered his head.

Sister Carol continued, " NOW LOOOORRRRRDD AH MIGHTY JEEESUS, LOOKIE DOWN HEEEERE AH, AT THIS HERE PLACE AND AH, GO GET MY DADDY TO AH RAIN SOME O' THAT DAMN FAR AN' HELL-NATION ON THESE BAD, BAD PEOPLE WHO GOT ME STOLE AH AND HID IN THIS HERE OLD DAMN HOUSE! . . . But not too much on my buddy Mark."

"Thanks," the Giant whispered.

"AN' DO IT QUICK AH ON ACCOUNT O' CHRISTMAS AN' ALL. YOU KNOW? AMEN, SAY AMEN!"

Mark stared wide-eyed at the door, then slowly toward the heavens and whispered, "Amen, . . . we're in for it now."

REVELATIONS

Wells spent an hour with Helen at the hospital. At first he was his pompous self, first giving the doctor the "are you doing all you can do" routine. Then started barking orders at the nurses.

Finally Helen spoke in her strong country accent. "Mr. Wells, they really have been treatin' Aunt Doreen with a lotta love and care. So don't ya be too hard on 'em."

He never lost stride. He walked over to Helen and whispered, "I guess this is my way of just getting things off my chest. Sort of takes my mind off worrying so much. I am sorry."

"Have ya heard anything on Carol?" Her eyes darted from one eye to the other searching for a sign.

"They called and want a ransom."

"I don't have much money."

"Oh, it's not much. I'll pay it, then we'll worry about the rest later."

"Do I need to be there?"

"I'll pick you up in the morning. Now I must run." Wells reached out and gave Helen's shoulder a gentle but awkward pat. He then walked over to one of the nurses and talked briefly. He turned toward Helen, mouthed a goodbye, waved and walked out. The nurse followed him out. She returned moments later with a leather suitcase for Helen. Wells had packed some of her things.

Later at his home, Wells looked across the desk at the smoking trooper. "We certainly had a bit of luck as far as the ransom amount is concerned."

"Why's that?" asked Coy.

"Well the amount was $250,000 and I had almost that much cash on hand in a safety deposit box. The banker agreed to forward $5,000 cash to me on my signature," said Wells.

"Do you have any other cash on hand?"

"Not in this county."

Coy watched the smoke draw over to the lamp shade then curl up through as though it were drawn through a smoke stack. He turned and stared hard at Wells. "How many people know what cash you got on hand!?"

"Why, just . . . Oh my God! It couldn't . . ."

"Who knew?"

"Just my accountant and my lawyer."

"Where's the accountant?"

"Married to my sister's niece," said Wells quietly, as though thinking aloud.

"Then we better talk to the lawyer, by God."

"Now?"

"No, it's too late. Let's let 'em hang theirselves . . . all of 'em. We'll be with 'em at that office in the mornin' first thing. We'll just reverse the ambush on 'em."

"I'll arrange it."

"I got some other bad news," said Coy.

"What now?"

"That crazy husband escaped from the Veterans hospital. It seems some nurse and this cop went talking about the kidnapping and they thought he was sleeping and anyway he's gone."

"I'll bet I know the nurse"

"What's that?

"Oh, another story, has he been spotted?" asked Wells.

"No"

"He can be a handful."

"How's that?"

"Well, I checked on him a bit and as it turns out, Mr. McMurfree is quite highly decorated black beret, a ranger. Do you know what that is?"

"Yeah, one of my former State Police partners was one. He was one, mean son of a bitch."

"Mr. McMurfree fits that description to the teeth. I had the opportunity to see him in action."

The trooper lit another cigarette and subconsciously lifted his hand to remove a bit of tobacco from his tongue, then he spoke, "Do you . . . ah . . "

"What?" said Wells, as he stared at the former trooper.

"Well, you wouldn't offer a feller a cup of coffee and shot o' bourbon would you?"

"I'd be delighted!" The old man smiled and seemed relieved that such a relaxing notion was suggested.

After the brewing was done. Wells carried a tray from the kitchen, then to the wet bar and finally arrived at his living room. He handed Coy the coffee in an imported mug and the bourbon in a leaded crystal tumbler.

Coy looked down at the arrangement, frowned and said, "Too much formality."

He then gulped half of the cup of coffee and poured the bourbon into the mug with the coffee.

Wells watched the arrangement with an amused frown, then he followed suit.

After a sip he looked up and said "Not bad."

"Did ya call the lawyer?" asked Coy.

"Yes, I told him I needed some last minute coaching on how to negotiate calmly."

The bourbon had a slow soothing effect on Coy's body but an immediate effect on his sense of humor and his mouth.

"You know Wells - I kinda like that about you."

"What's that?"

"You gotta lotta bull and a lotta balls."

"Why thank you officer. And I must say I find your demeanor adapts immediately to all situations," answered Wells.

"Thanks," the stare penetrated into Wells. "I think."

Wells stared through the window, into the cool evening.

"Something else botherin' ya," asked Coy.

"Well, yes. I still don't understand the child's obsession with the tree and the decorations and the whole Christmas event," said Wells.

"Did you ever ask her?" said Coy.

"Well, yes actually. Her answer was more of her usual holiday diatribe. She can be a brutal debater you know."

"I've witnessed that piece of her personality," said Coy.

"She probably never had to hear the word no like we have. I don't know about you, but for me, Christmas was just a day that we ate pie. Sometimes we had a tree. It was just a moment. When my wife was alive, it was an event, kinda like Carol's way."

"We usually had a small scrub of a tree on Christmas eve. It was a tradition of my Mother's family," answered Wells.

"Oh, you grew up poor too," answered Coy.

"Why do you say that."

"We got our tree on Christmas Eve because that's when they were free, or when they cost a nickel. You didn't ever figure that out?" asked Coy.

Wells stared at the old trooper for the longest time.

"I guess it never occurred to me then, or now I suppose. I thought it was my Mother's way. I suppose she was protecting us from harsher times," said Wells.

"People usually do the best that they can for those they love," answered Coy.

Wells finished his coffee and poured a little more bourbon into the cup. He turned back to the trooper.

"Well, we'd better call it a night, tomorrow may prove to be quite taxing."

"Yeah, business'll be pickin' up," agreed Coy.

RAGDOLL ANGEL

Coy thanked Wells for the drink as he made his departure. Wells watched him walk the length of the front walk - confident, wary. He reloaded the tray and walked toward the kitchen. Setting the tray on the table, he stared about. The house had never been this quiet. In the past few months the noise levels had reached an almost fever pitch and in the center of this life storm stood a tiny pile of awkward energy . . . with braids.

Wells exited the rear of the kitchen to the back hallway and pushed open the door to Doreen's room. When he hit the light switch, he was stunned by what he saw. Along the baseboard of two walls and organized to perfection were the decorations for the tree. Carol had watched the most famous home economist in America layout and decorate her tree on television. Carol had simply arranged the decorations and ornaments in order of attachment.

At the very end of the 'evergreen assembly line' and atop a small hatbox sat a cellophane fronted box that contained an angel. It was a handmade ragamuffin angel with dimples and a crooked smile and halo. The package read, 'The Littlest Angel'.

When Wells saw the angel, his mind's eye flashed to a scene of Carol on the front walk. She wore her winter coat with the fringe of her cowgirl dress extending from the bottom. Her western straw hat hung on her back by a red and white string and tied around her neck was the red bandana. Atop her braided hair sat an awkwardly pinned tinsel and wire halo.

Wells turned toward the door and tried to compose himself. He swallowed hard trying to remove the lump from his throat. He stopped at the door and held the switch for a few extra moments then, without looking back he turned off the light and closed the door. As he reached the top stair, he whispered a promise to himself.

"Tomorrow is a test I shall not fail."

Sleep came slow.

PALS

"Mark?"

"Yeah?"

"Would you open the door Pleeeease?"

Mark opened the door and stared down at the imp.

"I was wondering"

"What?"

"Well, since we're real good buddies now for a couple a' days, well, I was wondering. Well, you know, we played purty good all day an we had lunch together, an supper and even if you ain't a real good cook, but, well . . . "

"What?"

"Could I get a hug?" The big green eyes darted back and forth across the face looking for any sign or indication.

"Well, I guess it'd be OK."

At this point Carol was quite adept at explaining procedure to the gentle giant. "Kneel down more."

Mark grinned and knelt.

The little girl rushed forward and attempted to throw her arms around the hulking man-child. Instead her hand patted and squeezed both of Mark's arms.

"Hug me back, Mark."

The fingers of his left hand patted her gently on her entire back.

She looked up and smiled and gave him a peck on the cheek.

Then she pushed him up and grabbed his index finger and pulled him toward her sleeping room.

"What now?" asked Mark.

"Well, dammit, ya gotta tuck me in now, do I gotta tell ya everything."

"I guess," he replied smiling, then added, "Carol?"

"Yeah?"

"What would your Mommie say if she heard you cussin'?"

"Oh, I reckon I'd get a little tune up," she said smiling.

A little while later, Mark leaned against the edge of the small porch outside of the office. It was a night of the half moon with few clouds, the mountains in the distance bordered the wide night sky. He followed the stars to the horizon where he spotted the lights of a small hilltop farmhouse. He envisioned life within the house - a dad, a mom, and a child. He looked harder at the lights, trying to draw more of their lives into this notion. The vision vanished as tears blinded his sight.

"I'm sorry," he said. "I'm sorry."

AN AWAKENING

At 3:30 am Helen awoke and sat up on the edge of the hospital bed. Upon every awakening she felt disoriented. Then the smells and sounds brought back to her the reality. The acid taste came back to her mouth. She sipped some water and turned to see the nurse dozing in her chair. She smiled.

She turned toward Doreen and gasped. Doreen was staring at the ceiling as though dead in thought. Helen bounded toward the bed so quickly that she frightened her aunt.

Doreen slapped at Helen. "Cain't you see I'm a thinking!"

Helen beamed. "What are you thinking about, honey?"

Doreen stared into her eyes, "I think someone hit me." Then she cried silently. Neglecting her own tears, Helen blotted Doreen's tears as they ran down the eroded lines in the gentle old face.

After a while, Doreen stared into her niece's eyes then asked, "Helen?"

Helen replied softly, "Yes, yes, yes it's me Aunt Doreen, it's me, Helen." She leaned over and kissed Doreen gently on the cheek.

The strong old cleaning lady responded by hugging Helen hard enough to startle her. The nurse finally stirred. When she realized what had happened she ran from the room. Moments later, as the doctor was prodding Doreen and shining lights at her eyes, Helen called Wells.

"No, I don't think so, she barely remembers me."

"We should come down and question her, at once."

The force in Helen's voice ended Wells thoughts on this subject, "I'll not have you down here tormenting this woman right at this here moment Mr. Wells, sir. I'll just not have it."

"Well, uh, keep us posted if uh, there any more good news, OK?"

"I surely will."

"Goodbye then."

"Bye."

Wells called Coy and told him the news.

"It seems Doreen has come to," he began.

"Let's go. We'll question her."

"Well, Mrs. McMurfree doesn't think it's a good idea right now. Maybe later."

Sensing the tension in Wells' voice, Coy replied, " OK, we'll wait."

THE CALM

The temperature dipped suddenly. By nightfall Ted had found a good sleeping spot in a small culvert pipe but the cold air drove him further along into the night.

He had tried just stamping his feet to stay warm when this failed he ran head long into the night.

At a road crossing, the railroad company had built a small building to keep the switchman warm and dry as the trains changed directions. Although construction was consistent with all of their other buildings, it measured only four feet by four feet. Ted found the door unlocked. Inside he found a small oil heater and matches. After a few minutes he opened the window to cool down the over heated room.

He sat down in an ash armchair and slept fitfully. The imaginings and dreams were relentless, some rendered a fear of darkness, others brought back the battles. An unseen voice scolded him for allowing his family to be in this predicament. After three hours of this restlessness, Ted took possession of an old black denim railroadman's jacket, turned out the fire, closed the door and headed up the final grade.

He knew he was nearing Oak Hill. The engineer's signs along the track gave distances and more homes were built near the tracks. He walked under two coal tipples, each with a different coal company's name printed at the top with Oak Hill as the address. The steep grade, with its switchbacks and turns, took longer to climb.

At the mountain's top, the grade leveled. Ted sat for a moment to rest and watched dawn break over the mountains. From here, on this overcast December morning, the sun filtered through the gray fog like panes of frosted glass thawing from the night's chill, one by one, each throwing a spear of light through the brittle morning air.

As light broke above, Ted noticed lights coming on at the same time from the homes below. Twilight gripped the hills for the longest time, its shadow of darkness seemed to hold the day at bay. Ted shivered, maybe from the chill or maybe for fear of losing the darkness of night. It is so easy to hide there.

Without his notice of it, Ted's shivering slowed and stopped. He now had to squint to study the vale below. The sun was not blinding, but it warmed him and seemed to give him strength. He absent-mindedly brushed his pocket in hope of a bit more of Leon's cornbread.

Ted's eyes followed the rail line down toward the town. At the river the railroad forked. One side crossed a trestle and then north. The other went around the bend of the river toward the valley head.

From his vantage Ted also saw the highways into town. One road was parallel with the rail on which he stood and followed the ridge of the hill right into upper Oak Hill. This road continued on through and over then on toward Summersville where it intersected with Rainelle Pike. Lone cars softly hummed into and out of view, their tires whispering to the frosted highway. Morning had come.

Ted decided to stay on the rail. He had to get to Helen. He had to get his bearings. He was hesitant. He stared about again. Ted's eyes narrowed then he marched headlong down the grade and disappeared in the morning fog.

Coy walked out of his garage apartment, he stopped on the small gray porch to light his cigarette. He stared into the distance and he drank the last of his coffee, garnering strength for this day. He took the steep staircase two at a time and walked toward the Mercury. As he reached for the handle the gray Cadillac drifted down the alleyway and stopped beside him.

"Get in." said Wells.

Coy hopped on to the overstuffed wool flannel seat and glanced over his shoulder at Helen seated in the rear. She nodded her greeting, then focused through the front glass.

All were quiet as the huge car swung deftly onto Main Street.

Coy turned toward Helen, "How's your aunt this morning?"

"She's doing a lot better, thank ya."

Coy nodded smiling, then his face turned serious.

"Did Wells tell you 'bout your husband, ah, being missing from the hospital?"

"Yeah, he told me yesterday. I reckon he'll be along directly," she replied in a hushed voice as she continued to glare at the windshield.

Coy answered her reply with a puzzled stare.

THE STORM

The mood was quiet in the attorney's office. Wells started to speak, but Helen cut him off.

"So he said to be here."

"Yes," McKinley answered. His eyes were slightly glazed and cheeks a bit flushed from an attempt to relax with gin and tonics the previous evening.

"When did he say?" Helen continued.

"He didn't."

"Didn't you ask?"

"Well no . . ."

"Let's try to remain calm. We're all a little jumpy," said Wells in a grand, fatherly fashion. He even threw in a smile, as he went on, "Let's just thank the Lord that everything has worked out good so far."

This phrase helped Peter to relax but Helen and Coy shared a furrowed brow of puzzlement.

Then Wells continued, "Why we're just fortunate to have old Peter here to act as an intermediary with these culprits. Thank you very, very much for that Peter." Wells dropped his head as though humbled and extended his hand to Peter. Peter shook his hand, mouth agape, dumbstruck.

Helen's mouth hung open, as confused as the rest.

Well not all the rest. Coy sat down beside the metal trashcan, lit a cigarette and waited for the action to start.

Wells again continued, "Peter, I also need to thank you for helping us arrange the ransom payment. I just haven't been myself in as many days."

Wells shrugged, grimaced with lowered head and took the hand again.

Peter McKinney was completely at ease. He even stopped sweating.

"Peter?"

"Yes, sir?"

"Why is it that these kidnappers knew to the penny, the amount of cash on hand?"

"I beg your pardon… are you?… You're not suggesting that I could possibly be . . . "

"You bet you're sweet smelling, Yankee-educated ass I'm accusing you, you thieving bastard!"

"Mr. Wells, I'm not a fool! I may be naive at times but I'm not an idiot!"

"No one else knew!"

The room was completely quiet. Wells watched McKinney closely.

McKinney regained his composure, "Mr. Wells surely another member of your team was privy to this information."

"Don't think so."

"But you know confidentiality is of the utmost importance here."

"I don't think so!" Wells chanted again sternly.

"But Mr. Wells, I swear to you we've told no one."

"Who is we!"

"Why Miss Reed and…ah…. "

Wells head turned toward the secretary. When his eyes met hers, the reaction was immediate. Helen read it faster than either of the men. The chin thrust out proudly but the shoulders and neck cowered. Helen knew this standoffish posture. She knew hill people who displayed it in moments of triumph, regardless how hollow. Helen's childhood also afforded her the expertise with which to deal with these obstinate cowards.

Marguerite continued to stare defiantly back at Wells then she smiled congenially and said "Is there a problem I can help you with, Mr. Wells?"

Helen blindsided Marguerite. She grabbed a handful of hair at the nape of Marguerites neck and slammed her face into the desktop where she sat.

Coy quickly pulled Helen back to keep her from the kill but not before the secretary's head thumped the desk a second time.

Helen's intuition was quickly confirmed, "You gol'damn bitch!!" Marguerite shrieked through bloody teeth, "far as I'm concerned you'll never see that lil' bitch again."

Coy had to brace himself to hold Helen, whose left leg kicked at full stride, hitting Marguerette in the ribcage. The secretary winced as she half-spun in the oak chair.

Coy had his hands full. Helen was young, strong and mad enough to kill, and Marguerite sat there with a defiant smile decorating her stupid bloody, battered face. When Coy saw the smile, he was quite tempted to turn Helen loose. But the old coal operator took the lead in resolving this new twist.

Wells knew that the trump card was shifting back to the little tramp sitting at the desk. He also knew that she was from a rough breed and they would gain nothing from physical torture. He couldn't let her take the upper hand.

Wells reached to his back waist and withdrew a nickel-plated, pearl handled Browning 45 automatic pistol. He chambered the first shell loudly as he looked at Marguerite.

"Hell, this worthless piece of trash is used to getting her ass kicked. Let's see how she handles this," he shouted.

He raised the pistol at her and fired. The first round tore through the door casing three feet to her right. The second shattered a picture to her left. He continued walking toward her cussing loudly. The third round took the mail tray from her desk and sent paper flying straight to the wall. The fourth round plowed through the veneer almost in front of Marguerite. Splinters from the desk hung out of her now bleeding arm.

Wells, now on top of Marguerite leveled the smoking weapon at her chest. He leered at the now shocky secretary.

"Who has her!" he screamed.

"Artie! Artie! Artie!" she cried.

"Where does he have her!" barked Wells.

"I swear I don't know."

Wells pulled the gun up to her eye.

"At some old mine, that's all I know."

"Well hell – there's probably fifteen old mines around here," he said, looking at Coy. He turned suddenly back to the secretary and brushed the barrel of the gun slowly across her trembling lips.

She pulled her hands up to protect herself.

"How are they going to contact us?" he said calmly.

"He'll call. LLLet ya talk to the kid," Marguerite whimpered.

Coy spoke, "Let Helen take the call." Then he turned to Helen. "You'll have to control the conversation when you talk to Carol. This guy still thinks Carol is 'his' daughter," Coy said pointing to Wells.

"I understand."

Coy glanced over at McKinney, "You look kinda pasty, boy. You all right?"

Peter couldn't answer. He just nodded.

"Whose supposed to answer the phone," Wells yelled at Marguerite.

"He didn't say," answered the secretary.

"OK."

Wells stared hard at the secretary, then McKinney, then the phone, then at everyone again. He scratched his forehead with the gun barrel.

Coy smoked quietly and watched the tension mount. He wasn't too worried about Wells. The old man was radical but always in control. He watched Helen more carefully.

If he hadn't grabbed her just moments ago, he knew the secretary would be dead or near death.

Coy weighed all the facts then spoke. "When they call, they'll expect you to answer." He began, directing the statement to Marguerite. "Now if you let him know that we're onto 'em or if I think you're warning him, I'm gonna let these two take turns at ya'.

Do you realize how serious that could be?"

The secretary curled her upper lip and mocked Coy. "Yeah, I realize how goddamn serious it is."

The old trooper took a long step forward and slapped the heel of his left hand into the flesh of the tramp's mouth.

"Now if I think Mr. Wells and Mrs. McMurfree aren't serious enough for ya', well then I'll just have to join in too. I don't hit women as a rule but in your case I'll make an exception. Now do you realize how serious this is?" he growled.

Marguerite saw a flash of light when the old trooper hit her, then came nausea, then she came around again, finally realizing that all paths of retreat were gone, she nodded.

"OK, then straighten yourself up a little bit an' get ready to take your phone call."

The secretary nodded again. She opened the drawer to her left and withdrew a small mirror, then after a good look, she began dabbing a tissue about her battered face with a trembling hand as she sniffled and sniveled.

"You know Mark," Carol began, with still a few corn flakes in her mouth. "I sure miss my mama, but I'm likin' not having to take a bath and I don't miss that."

Marked smiled nervously. He knew Artie was due.

"Sometimes, I like to have a bath," he said

"Aunt Doreen says ya gotta get a bath aw'most every day or you'll get cobwebs up yer butt. Do you ever get cobwebs up yer butt, Mark?" asked Carol.

"Uh uh, I don't know."

"Ain't ya never looked?" she added.

"What? Ah, . . . no."

"Me neither, come to think about it."

Carol choked down the last of the cornflakes in the milk, then threw down the spoon and drank the bowl.

The door opened, Artie came in shivering. "Jesus Christ it's cold out there. You got her ready yet."

"Almost."

Carol scowled at Artie.

Artie scowled back, then laughed.

"Hey Mark, make some coffee."

Mark already had it brewed. He poured the cup and passed it to Artie.

Artie walked over to the box stove and warmed his backside as he sipped the hot coffee. "Thanks, old buddy, God, it's gonna be a lovely day."

Artie kept humming as he drank the coffee and ate a baloney sandwich.

"All right Mark, get her jacket on her and let's git!" Artie barked.

The truck drifted quietly on to the narrow blacktop highway and Artie pushed the shifter up into second and headed toward Thurmond. Four miles later, Artie drifted the truck into a small Mobil service station. The small white clapboard station touted the famous winged red horse above the 'Mobil' name. On the right side of the station house stood a drive-on service rack built from heavy creosoted timbers with a pair of metal ramps to drive onto for oil changes and such. On the left of the station stood a 'his and hers' outhouse. It had a sloping tarpaper roof and was whitewashed to match the station house.

The owner came out, smiled and said "Filler up?"

"Yeah, long as it don't cost more'n two dollars," replied Artie with a laugh. "Hey Bud, you gotta pay phone, don't ya'."

"Yeah, on the side," the cheerful full-service smile was gone.

Artie held Carol's hand and pulled her roughly toward the phone. He threw the dime into the slot.

Marguerite picked up the phone and as cheerfully as she could, stated, "Peter J. McKinney, Attorney at Law, may I help you? One moment please."

Marguerite held the phone toward Wells, "He wants to talk to you."

Coy grabbed the phone, held his hand over the receiver, then whispered some quick instructions to Helen then handed her the phone.

Helen needed no other prompting, "I know you wanted to talk to Thad but please let me talk to Carol first, then I let ya talk to him. Please…please?"

"All right, but make it quick."

Artie stooped and looked hard at Carol, "I'm gonna let you talk to your mama so don't try any o' yer smart-ass lil' tricks."

"Yes sir."

"Here."

Carol took the phone and smiled at Artie then said "Hello."

"Carol, are you OK?"

"I'm fine 'cept I'm real tired of corn flakes and baloney and I need to watch some TV, and how's Aunt Doreen and this one guy's kinda nice and the other one is kind of a butt hole an'..."

Artie whispered an oath as he snatched the phone from Carol's hand and started to backhand her. Artie swung hard but his arm wouldn't move. He looked back and Mark had a grip on his coat that simply allowed no movement of his arm.

"You said you wasn't gonta hurt her," said Mark, in a strained quivering voice.

"Alright, already, let me go. I won't hit her," said Artie in an equally bitter voice.

The huge man-child let him go and still held his arms out as if Artie might change his mind.

Artie whipped the receiver to his mouth, "Was that enough to satisfy you?"

"Yes that will be satisfactory for now," said Wells. "Just remember what I told you on our last conversation."

"She ain't gotta hair outta place," said Artie.

"How do we get the money to you?" said Wells.

"Well sir, you just get in that big ole Cadillac of your'n and head on down towards Cunard. Know where at is, don't cha," said Artie.

"Yes"

"OK, there's a gas station there, half way up the grade. Little Mobil station. Out back in the out house behind the gas station there's a note behind the up vent stack."

"OK. I'm following you," said Wells.

"The note'll tell ya where the trade is. If I see the troops with ya, the girls mine," said Artie.

"I understand," said Wells.

"You'll have to leave now to make it on time."

"OK then," said Wells.

"Alone."

"Of course."

Coy listened intently as Wells repeated the instruction of the kidnapper.

Coy asked, "Is that Cunard Road the one where the coal truck went over the hill last spring?"

"Yes, yes I believe you're right."

"I was out there. That road follows the base o' that rock cliff for four miles. He picked a good road to study the car and make sure you're alone," said Coy.

"That's what I was thinking."

"Where's this gas station at?" asked Coy.

"Actually it's just up the grade a little way from where the accident occurred."

"Well you better get going."

"OK, I think I have everything," said Wells.

"Hey, Wells."

"Yes?"

"If the opportunity arises, don't try any more o'that Wyatt Earp bullshit, alright."

The old man frowned, picked up the satchel and said, "No, not until we get Carol back." He nodded and left.

Moments later the sheriff picked up Marguerite with Coy's instructions. As an after thought Coy told Sheriff Boyce to take McKinney with him.

"The pathetic looking son of a bitch bears watchin'. Better call his wife."

Coy and Helen decided to wait at the intersection of Route 19 where State Route 409 heads toward Cunard. Coy parked the lawyer's Studebaker off the road then the two got out and paced like sentries.

Coy quizzed Helen about the kidnappers. Just in case he missed something, and also to help her to occupy her mind.

"You seen these guys before?"

"Yeah"

"Where?"

"Aunt Doreen pointed 'em out one night down at the Fireman's Fair. She called 'em the two town idiots. I asked her which was which and she says it didn't matter, one was dumb as the other."

"How's Doreen this morning?"

"Pretty confused still."

"If anything starts happening out here, don't start actin' like no damn banty rooster again, alright?"

She put her hands on her hips and stared hard at the old state trooper, then seemed to focus into the distance down that road to Cunard.

Crazy women scare the hell outta me, he thought. *They always did and they always will.*

THE DROP......................REALLY

Following the train tracks down this last mountain had been hard. Ted had crossed three short trestles, all ice covered and with no handrail to boot. He had crossed the freshly oiled timbers on the trestles stiff legged and slow. When he reached the valley floor, he found the grade long and flat, it seemed to go on and on. At times he was tempted to climb the hill and take to the highway, but he just wasn't sure if he was ready to face people yet.

Ted's pace was picking up. After three days on the rails, the length of his stride had adjusted to automatically put his heal on every other the tie. He had even worked out the rhythm for a cadence to occupy his mind. He marched on, toward Oak Hill, chanting the cadence with his breath.

"Oh shit!"

Ted bounded off the rails to the side brush and looked down the track approximately three hundred yards. There on the track a tall man stood, waiting, and looking all about. Ted lowered his body tightly to the ground and crawled along silently, maneuvering for a better position to watch the man on the tracks.

The Cadillac pulled into the small service station half way up the grade toward Cunard. Wells stepped out of the car wearing a full length Harris Tweed and a felt Stetson. He smiled at the attendant, a greasy faced boy with a shy and unintelligent demeanor.

Wells handed the kid a five and asked, "Where's the bathroom son?"

The kid replied, "I'd be happy to tell ya the location of that bathroom if you'd tell me the location of where ya put the gas in this here thing."

Wells pushed the button on the tail light, revealing the gas cap, then headed for the out building.

Wells entered the outhouse and so as not to miss a thing, he scanned the walls in a slow sweeping motion. The wind wasn't as cold but whistled through each batten board creating an odd harmony.

He reached behind the vent stack and withdrew the letter. It was written on the bonded stationary of Peter J. McKinney. Wells' thoughts were racing. He knew this man had either anticipated their finding his accomplice in McKinney's office or simply didn't care if they had. This letter was the final proof of an advantage turned sour. The kidnapper did not care for the safety of his accomplices and probably not the safety of the child.

Wells walked back toward the Caddy. As he approached, the attendant joked about the hidden gas cap on his 'modern' automobile.

"If they keep hidin' trap doors on these here Cadillacs, we fellers won't know how to even get inside these dang things, huh."

Wells replied with a frown, being of no heart to be amused.

"Hey Mister, it only took two dollar and twenty cent."

"Keep the change," he replied flatly.

Wells pulled the keys from his pocket and opened the trunk and withdrew the heavy leather bag. He closed the trunk lid and as instructed in the letter, he walked across the roadway to the guardrail where the red bandana was tied, and threw the bag over the steep embankment. He walked back over to the Cadillac, slid behind the wheel and started the engine. He watched the clock on the dashboard helplessly. The note said to wait fifteen minutes and any deviation would result in the child's death. His watch seemed to be running slower than the dash clock. He focused on his wristwatch. He felt helpless.

Ted watched the big man for several minutes and as he kept his eyes on the man, he crept nearer, first standing just below the rail then creeping forward a bit and kneeling in broom straw, then sprinting quickly along the tracks.

After another ten minutes had passed, Ted was within seventy yards of this huge man. He felt this to be a good vantage point and was near enough to see and hear the man on the tracks without being seen. He had found good cover in a clump of sage, briar, and rock. The man started walking back and forth, continually looking up.

Suddenly Ted heard a noise from up above.

The big man reacted at the same moment. He jumped into an eager sort of stance and stared upward. Together they saw the object coming over the hill from above. Ted watched as the giant shifted left, then right, then centered and tried to catch the brown rolling object. It was just too heavy. The big man opened his arms and was promptly driven into the ground.

Ted was astounded. He imagined the big man was as well. The giant slowly lifted himself then fell over again. He did this three times and spilled back over three times.

Finally the giant was able to stand, although dazed. The giant started to spin in a circle, trying to focus. He came about to face Ted's direction, stunned. He looked toward Ted in a caricature of slack shoulders, heaving chest, bloody nose and slightly unfocused eyes.

Ted laughed aloud, then quickly ducked into the brush and giggled silently. This small noise brought the giant quickly out of his stupor. He shook his head, turned, and picked up the brown satchel and ran down the tracks.

Ted followed, quickly, but out of sight. It was hard to keep up at first, the man moved fast. As he ran, he would stumble, fall, and yelp like a child, then strut forward again, holding the satchel to his chest. When he tried sprinting again, the cycle would repeat itself. The commotion allowed Ted to keep up, unnoticed.

Ted was so busy studying the movements of the huge man, he didn't notice the pickup truck sitting fifty yards ahead on the gravel beside the rails. The giant's pace slowed until a sharp voice came from the truck.

"Get your ass in here." On command, the giant ran and hopped in the front seat.

Ted watched the truck spinning and sinking into the loose fill gravel. Gradually it started to move, slowly. A narrow embankment ran parallel with the rail line at this point and Ted found it easier to run along the top of this embankment. It gave him a better view of the truck and its occupants. When he was within twenty yards of the truck, he saw the giant hanging out the window, watching the rear tires work then turn and give his report to the driver. Ted was fifteen yards from the truck and looking down from the embankment. As he studied the driver, he could only see the driver's angry, venom-spewing, twisted mouth from his vantage point. What he saw he did not like.

The truck stopped. It had slid dangerously close to the edge of a steeper bank.

The truck's engine idled, easing the truck slowly down the grade. The giant man's head and torso hung from the window to watch the truck's progress. A small head popped up to look as well.

Ted froze then bolted toward the truck. He had come to be with Helen and see if he could help somehow. Why was she here? Was it Carol?

> The truck's engine raced for a moment. Artie dropped the shifter down into low and revved the engine and kicked out the clutch. The truck seemed to hover, unmoving. Artie cursed loudly and stopped. He then slipped the clutch lightly so the over-acceleration wouldn't bury the truck into the loose gravel again. It worked, but he couldn't go fast. Ted listened to the cursing as the pickup put distance between them again.

Ten minutes at normal speed to freedom and wealth, thought Artie.

"Son of a Bitch!" he fumed. The truck was too heavy for this stretch of track.

THE GETAWAY

Wells let the second hand sweep an extra thirty seconds past the fifteen minutes for good measure. The Cadillac rolled quietly onto the roadway. Wells drove slowly at first. It was as though the Cadillac was trying to walk quietly by what evil lurked below the cliff at the road's edge.

His mind raced, pondering what was happening below. He knew the briefcase dropped down a sheer cliff onto a rail line below. He was trying now to imagine the escape route. If they followed the line west, it led to State Route 38 but it would be a long slow trip. If they followed the line east, it would run right into Oak Hill.

Wells had decided the escape route into Oak Hill was the option that the kidnappers would choose. He fought desperately to keep his foot off the accelerator. At one point, Wells pumped the brakes to slow the car almost to a stop. Wells knew that anxiety was completely non-productive. He considered this for a moment and replaced his anxiety with anger. This suited him much better. Easier to control! He reached back to the holster under his jacket and let his fingers brush the handle of the Browning. He repeated this movement until it became a natural reflex.

The truck stopped suddenly. "What's a matter?" Mark asked.

"I heard a noise from one of the tires." he replied. "Why don't you get out and check it out?"

"Well, uh what do I check for?"

"You'll know when ya see it." Mark stepped out of the truck with a puzzled look on his face.

"Go on around to the back a ways and squat down 'an see if ya see anything on the inside of the back tires, now, an' hurry. It ain't like we got a lot 'o time. Now git."

Mark stomped past the truck and squatted down just in time to see the gravel roll off the back tires. He jumped up and trotted after the truck. Carol looked back at the stumbling, falling giant waving his arms and giving chase. Then she glared up at the grinning madman who hung on the steering wheel of the truck.

"Hey you forgot Mark!" Carol barked.

"Don't need him anymore lil' darling, and as a matter of fact, your usefulness is getting' less important all the time."

Mark was confused. Then he looked up and saw the roadway above him. He knew Artie would be coming by on the road just as soon as he pulled up off the tracks.

Mark hurried down off the gravel, through the brush and then started clawing his way up the sharp incline toward the highway. After falling part way back down only once, Mark worked his way to the top and stepped across the mesh wire guardrail on to the blacktop. He didn't know which way to go, so he went left, then right then both ways again. Finally he went toward where he thought the pickup might go. Right.

COLD TRAILIN'

Ted stopped, dropped to a squatting position and started taking deep breaths. The South Koreans had taught him to rest in this fashion and it quickly released the pressure from his throbbing muscles. After just a minute or two, Ted hopped up and started walking until his muscles were loose again. He eased back into his soft trot.

Entering the downgrade, Ted broke his concentration of staring down at the railroad ties to see if he could catch sight of the truck. Instead, he caught a glimpse of the giant, arms flailing about wildly. Ted lost his footing for a second. After regaining his balance, he looked again and the giant was gone.

Now the glimpses weren't confusing him. They were angering him. His pace quickened. Ted ran to where he thought he saw the giant. Here he found tire tracks. He held his breath and listened intently for any sound of a child. There were none. Again, he ran after the truck.

Wells pulled off the road at the intersection. He looked up to see Helen pacing back and forth and Coy blowing cigarette smoke out slowly. Coy had already read Wells' face and knew the situation. Helen glanced up as briefly from her post, then walked over long enough to listen to Wells relate the frustration of the money drop. After his description of the drop and then as he alluded to his ride back to the intersection, Helen walked back. She tried to imagine not feeling so helpless.

The intersection of Cunard Road and the Oak Hill Road occurred in the middle of a horseshoe turn. The roadway bent around a hill with the intersection facing the steep slope.

Wells and Coy stood in the shade of the hill while Helen paced about on the outside of the turn on the opposite side of the highway. Helen could pace one way and then the other with the advantage of a good view in all three directions. That's why she saw the giant first.

She was so blind with rage that Mark was merely seventy-five yards from the intersection before she spotted him. At first glance she just discounted him as a passerby, when he stumbled and teetered, she eyed him more closely.

When he was fifty yards from her, she recognized him from her encounter at the Fair with Doreen. Helen ran as fast as a gossip whisper across the road to meet the giant head on. Mark studied the road and didn't see the little lady run, headlong, over to intercept him. Only Coy at the last second noticed Helen sprinting out of view down the road to his left.

All Mark heard was "You son of a bitch" before the bony small fist buried itself into his already broken nose. He saw a bright light, then only tears for several seconds. He held his arms up to protect himself from the flurry of punches. As his eyes cleared, he saw the small woman before him. He started to reach out as the foot met his groin. His chin fell to his chest, then the foot came up again, harder.

Mark fought nausea, and then dropped to one knee. He heard other voices. He hoped they would stop the woman.

As his vision cleared this time he saw her pick up a large rock and start back toward him. Mark whimpered and started to cower toward the ground.

A large foot hit his chest and he flew backward, his head hitting the pavement.

He blacked out momentarily. As he came to and stirred, the foot came to rest on his chest. He looked up to see the old trooper pointing a finger down at him.

"Stay put, you son of a bitch!" Somehow Mark was relieved to be held down.

Then, resting his foot on the giant's chest, Coy turned his attention toward the others. His voice was loud and sharp, and he startled everyone. "Put down that goddamn rock and Wells, you can holster that goddamn pistol! You two lunatics are coming near to going to jail yourselves. Do you wanna keep that damn whore from

McKinney's office company down at the jail? Now damn-it to hell you're getting on my damn nerves hand!"

Helen slammed the rock into the hillside, and then strutted toward Coy, pushing her coat sleeves up as she came. Wells lowered the gun but kept it in his hand. The old trooper looked from felon to friend with the same furrowed brow then without warning he immediately spun and dropped his right knee into the giants chest.

"Listen hard you big dumb bastard. Where's Carol?"

"She's wif Artie . . . ah."

"Where they going?"

"I don't know, and . . . "

"Well what!"

"An' . . . uh, uh. Artie missed the turn off an', an' he didn't care."

"What turn off?" said Coy.

"The one that brings you up here, onto this road," said Mark.

Coy looked toward Wells, "Where's that rail line end up?"

"It runs right into Oak Hill then crosses the river to a spur line to Charleston."

"Can that truck cross that bridge?" asked Coy.

"Of course not, it's ballasted," replied Wells.

"What the hell's ballasted mean?" said Coy.

The bridge has its support superstructure below the rail," explained Wells. "The rails are then bedded in stone much like a normal ground rail system. Why it's even difficult to walk on it if the stone is new and it is. As a matter of fact it's heaped up fairly high"

"Thanks for the lesson, professor. There has to be another way out," said Coy.

"There's an old construction road entrance if it's still passable. They tried to construct a tunnel there in '39 and it didn't work. You see, they..."

"Save it - let's go!"

It seemed safer with Wells and Helen in the front and the giant in the back seat next to Coy. Mark tried to doctor his bloody nose with cuffed hands and a tissue he'd found in the back seat.

Wells spoke again, "You know to get there, we have to go to Oak Hill, then out toward the grave yard, then down toward the river."

"So"

"As the crow flies they are probably almost there."

"Damn!"

VANISHING POINT

Ted was weak, but his feet kept pounding against the railroad ties. He tried to set an easier cadence as he kicked in pursuit of the truck. As soon as he adjusted to his pace and stride, he reached his legs farther toward the slowly disappearing truck, toward his daughter.

Then the truck slowed and stopped.

Ted's wobbling legs steadied as he eyed the now stopped truck. He knew the face was Carol's. Now, as he raced wildly for the pickup, he somehow thought it might be a wishful thought. But his doubts weren't translated to his feet. They slapped hard against the rail ties. Ted's feet pounded harder, but the truck just seemed to float farther - and farther down the track away from him. The cramps came quicker this time. The empty stomach throbbed, the chest burned, and the heart pounded. The truck was just fifteen yards moments before, and now it was 500 yards, then more.

ONLY THE TOUGH SURVIVE

"I'll tell ya something kid - you're kinda entertainin' an' all but if you don't stop cussin me, I'm gonna lay hands on you. Do you understand me?" Artie held Carol off the seat by her hair - then dropped her as he continued driving.

It was hard for Carol to give him a dirty look with tears in her eyes. "Asshole," she whispered.

"What?!" Artie had seen her lips move.

"Nothing."

Artie smacked the top of her head.

She lay against the door, listening to the harsh, hysterical laughter.

"Well by damn, we made it," said Artie.

Carol looked out the window at the tin wall beyond the front of the truck. She quickly rubbed her arm over her face to dry the tears and her running nose. She wouldn't give Artie the satisfaction of hearing or seeing her cry.

The cadence of running down the track turned natural again. When Ted lost concentration, his heel would fall short of the tie and the end result was a bone-jarring event. The concentration kept his mind off of the pain. Occasionally a dreamy euphoria took over. He fought it by stopping, composing for a moment, and cursing it away. When the euphoria evolved into pain and nausea, Ted slowed his pace to a walk. He wouldn't stop. He knew how feeble he must appear - stumbling along at a snails pace.

The track bowed around the hill at a slight decline, and Ted felt every change in grade acutely. As the rails straightened Ted saw the track turn and cross the river on a bridge. He stopped and stared hard. No truck could cross that thing. He walked closer studying the gravel for signs of the truck. He then saw what he believed were tire tracks. He walked slowly now, studying the ground.

Ted stood at the outside of the curve, pacing slightly to keep his muscles loose. He stared out across the bridge. It would take a miracle to cross the bridge in a truck and almost as bad on foot. But the gravel showed no sign of any traffic. He turned and stared at the way he'd come. He could clearly see the tire trails coming right at him. Ted followed them and suddenly turned 180 degrees and saw where the tire trail had veered sideways into the brush.

Ted walked through the waist high brush until it led him fifty yards ahead onto a graveled roadway. As he stared ahead down the hill, the roadway followed the curve of the hill toward some sort of tin building. It stood two hundred yards away.

Ted paced cautiously toward the tin. The tire tracks turned sharply toward the right. Ted followed. He stopped suddenly and saw the bumper of the truck projecting up out of the water. He froze momentarily then slid and shuffled down the rocky riverbank toward the water. At the bottom, he couldn't stop himself and ran headlong into the icy water.

The steel gray sky reflected off the water, but as Ted stood chest deep in the river, he could see through and into the truck - no one was there. After the shock of the cold water wore off, it actually soothed his aching muscles but quickly started to sap his strength.

Ted splashed feverishly toward the shore. He fought his way up the mud-slicked river edge and back up the rocky bank. With hands bleeding and fear subsiding, Ted scanned the bank down the river in hopes of spotting the child. He turned about as he walked around looking for a roadway, path, or just some sign. Helplessness overwhelmed him. He found himself suddenly fifty yards from a high, corrugated tin wall, probably fencing in an old mine or quarry.

BUSTIN' OUT

Artie smiled down at the little moppet beside him in the seat of the Ford. His eyes rolled as the warm beer washed another pill down his throat.

"You know something, lil' darling. I been calculating here, an' near as I can figure, our age difference is about the same as your ol' daddy Wells and your Momma. So I don't see no reason why we can't be friends. Hell, we'll be more n' friends. Heh, heh, heh."

The tiny redneck looked up at Artie and said, "Mr. Wells ain't my daddy!"

"He paid your ransom."

"He ain't my daddy."

"Don't matter," Artie slurred, "I ain't your daddy either."

Artie turned the key and the Ford roared to life. He dropped the shifter into drive and inched toward the tin until it made contact, then accelerated slightly and watched the loosely nailed tin fall forward. As the daylight poured into the cave, the brightness caused him to squint. As he focused through his narrowed eyes, he thought he saw the outline of a man. "What's that?"

"What?" answered Carol.

As the Ford inched through the opening in the wall, it suddenly snagged a piece of tin. Artie hung his head out the window and stared down, "Well shit!"

He backed up then slapped the shifter into park and opened his door. "Sit still, you little bitch!" he barked.

He slammed the door and started tugging the tin sheets to clear a path for the car.

"Mister?"

"What the fu . . . " Artie spun to strike only to feel his right arm snap and fall helplessly to his side. He raised the left to counter, it only appeared as if the stranger's hand slapped his hand but the same thud and snap followed and the left arm fell limp to his side. Artie howled in pain and rage.

"You son of a ..." he began.

The soldier answered Artie's slur by pivoting his body and sending an elbow into Artie's chin. Artie rolled over the hood and up the window and comically stared at Carol, then rolled unconsciously onto the ground.

Carol studied the dirty, stubble-faced creature before her.

"Hey, Punkin," he whispered.

Carol jumped through the open door and studied the odd man before her for only a few seconds.

"Daddy!"

Ted held out an arm and the little girl swung into the crook of his right arm and threw her arms around his neck.

He was startled by the tenderness of the little warm nose against his neck. His back straightened and stiffened, but the little giggling head against his neck made his lips curl into a smile.

"How'd ya find me Daddy?" asked the child.

"Oh, ah, I jus' come this way ."

"Good Finkin'!"

They were walking back up the grade when Ted saw the road leading up toward the highway above. Within a minute he could see the post and steel net guardrail above him.

Wells didn't slow the Deville down as he entered the town. He had planned the trip through Oak Hill precisely. The Caddy didn't drop below 50 mph, nor did he stop for signs, or consider one-way streets valid. Mark shook in the back seat while the others leaned forward.

The trooper watched Mark closely but still held onto the passenger strap on the doorpost to keep from rolling as Wells took the turn onto Main at fifty-five miles per hour. When he passed under Oak Hill's only red light the speedometer read seventy-five. Coy gave Mark a double take when he heard that one single word from the giant.

"Hurry."

Forty-two seconds after entering the city, the Cadillac crested the hill and began the steep incline down toward the river. The car, airborne for just seconds, barked its tires like a landing passenger plane as the car met the roadway. Now Wells concentrated hard on the access road leading down to the railroad.

"Well shit!" yelled Wells. He locked up the brakes as he slid past the entrance to the maintenance road. The tires squealed as he backed up. The Cadillac stopped, then turned toward the road entrance, then stopped again. Wells threw the car into park and started to draw the pistol, yet again.

Coy had one foot out the door, pistol in hand when Helen flew past him. "Crazy Bitch is at it again," he whispered as he bolted after her. He unconsciously holstered his pistol as he saw Helen unite with her family. He looked over at Wells who was leaning against the open door, smiling.

"Do I need to ask who that is?" asked Coy.

"That would be Carol's father."

"How'n the hell'd he git here?" Coy asked. Wells shrugged.

The man-child cuffed in the back seat of the Cadillac smiled, nodding his head several times, not knowing how, but certainly knowing why. He remembered the little girl's prayer for her Father to come to her rescue. He knew in his heart as well, that somewhere on those railroad tracks below, “damn far and hell-nation” had been rained hard upon his cousin Artie.

BACK TO BUSINESS

The McMurfree family continued their reunion back in Wells' home. Helen bathed and then quizzed Carol to make sure she was not wounded in any way, shape, or form. As her mother lovingly performed her inspection, she answered an onslaught of questions from Carol about the condition of her Aunt. Despite her mother's reassurances, the small brows created an arch of introspection. Ted found clean clothes in the trunk Helen brought from Otter Holler, then showered in Doreen's bathroom. Afterward, he waited with Wells and Coy in the kitchen.

Thirty minutes later, as father, mother, and child entered the hospital ward, the bond between Doreen and the child was revealed to all. As Carol let go of her mother's hand and rushed toward her aunt, Doreen threw the covers aside and spun in the bed. Carol quickly climbed the side rails and landed on her knees in front of Doreen. She reached gently to the bandages on Doreen's head.

"Are you OK, Aunt Doreen?" asked the child softly as she touched the head wrap.

"I'm gonna be just fine honey. How 'bout you? That son of a . . . ah, gun hurt you any?"

"Nah, not me, and he ain't a son 'o gun." Carol leaned closer. "He's a son o' bits."

"I know honey," said Doreen, pulling Carol in for her hug.

"Wait a minute! What day is this?" Carol blurted out. Then stared up at the nurse for the answer.

"Why…well it's Wednesday afternoon, December nineteenth, sweetie."

" Then how many days 'til Christmas is it?" barked Carol.

"It would be five days until Christmas eve, but . . ." the nurse replied.

"Thanks. Aunt Doreen, we gotta git you outta here, we got things to do. We gotta get that tree up and then get those presents for you know who," she said winking as she began lifting fingers for each item on her to-do list.

Carol faced Doreen and nodded her head back toward her

mom "An' I think maybe we gotta get you-know-who-else, something else." She'd said winking wildly. "When you gonna get out?"

The nurse interrupted, "Now sweetie your aunt is going to have to stay for some more rest, so you'll have to make other plans, and I also think . . ."

"Well shit! Whoops. That just slipped out." Carol blurted out as she held her hands up. Then, looking up to Wells, she said, "Well, I guess it's me and you, Mr. Wells!"

"Well allright, then."

"Mind if I tag along," Coy added softly from the doorway.

"Well, come on deputy!" Carol yelled. "The more the merry."

Wells glanced over at Helen, "We'll get her back in just a little while so you won't get too . . . ah, anxious."

Helen smiled and nodded, "Carol?"

Carol ran back and Helen picked her up and traded hugs, then leaned toward her father to land a kiss then leaned back. Helen said, "You know the rules?"

"Right," Carol whispered, "Get Mr. Wells back by three o'clock for his nap so he don't get too cranky."

"That's it. Be good."

"Bye."

Carol never looked back.

Carol held Wells' hand and was heading for the car when she spotted two county deputies leading Mark and Artie toward the Ford cruiser in the drive. Artie's arms had been cast and Mark's head cut was taped.

Carol looked up at Wells. "I gotta tell Mark something." She pulled him toward the cruiser.

"Hey Mark," she yelled toward the window.

Mark smiled and searched for the window crank but it was gone.

Coy reached forward and opened the door halfway. "She wants to tell you something, boy. Just make sure you don't try nothing."

Carol looked up soberly and replied, "OK."

"Hi . . . hi, ah, hi, Carol."

"Hey Mark, Merry Christmas."

"Merry Christmas, ah, to you, Carol," said the giant with eyes glistening.

"Now Mark, I reckon you're gonna go to the jail or something and I just wanted to thank you for being my friend." She smiled and waved her fingers bye.

Artie leaned over in his narcotic stupor and winked. Carol jumped back from the door. Artie hung over further, "Come back over here, darling. Hey! What about me and you? Weren't we meant to be together, damnit?"

Mark pushed Artie back to the far side of the seat, away from Carol. Artie's cuffed hands and freshly plastered arm-casts rattled against the far door.

"It's not right to talk to a little girl like 'at," said Mark.

Artie stared at Mark, then grinned and said, "Well look at you, you big dumb baby. That little bitch got you piss-eyed crying. What you do to my poor cousin you little bitch."

Artie was leaning again, almost on top of Mark.

Mark swung his cuffed arms to the right then fiercely to the left. His left elbow caught Artie in the chin. Artie's head cracked the safety glass then ricocheted back toward Mark, when Mark connected the second time, Artie's head penetrated the side glass of the Ford and lodged into the broken safety glass. He dangled there, unconscious.

Just then the police band radio cracked to life. "This here's the Sheriff. What the hell's a taking so long with them pris'ners."

Deputy Merrit leaned over and picked up the mike. "This here's Deputy J.C. Merritt. Hey sheriff, that one prisoner just attempted to escape. He was fairly unsuccessful in this attempt, but it seems we gotta take him back in the damn hospital and git him sewed up agin."

"Good job, men!"

As she walked toward the Cadillac with Wells and Coy, Carol looked back. The two friends, one - a small child, the other - a gentle giant, waved goodbye one last time.

EPILOG

A short time of healing had come and gone. The housekeeper had come home in time for Christmas. The young husband and father had finally found his way back home from his war.

The lawyer's secretary was recovered from her physical encounter, though her mental outlook was still a bit skewed. Artie was recovering from his broken arms, dislocated shoulder, and head contusions as well as could be expected until Wells showed the old trooper the bruises on Carol's head.

When Coy saw the marks on the child's head, he reached to move the fine strawberry blond hair to see more clearly, and that is when he saw the bruising and felt the bumps. The old trooper curled the knuckle of his index finger and gently touched the dimple on her right cheek. Carol responded with a smile. Coy walked the long hallway from Wells' kitchen, exited the house, walked right past his car and walked the full mile to the jail. If you had passed him that day it may have frightened you to see his lips forming words, horrible words, and the tear in the corner of his eye.

Entering the jail, Coy walked past the Sheriff and into the lock-up. He walked up to the bars that held Artie and quietly asked, "I'll bet you wouldn't give a damn if you didn't see me for a couple a' days, would ya'?"

"By God, you musta read my mind you tin star asshole," he slurred, adding a few disgusting epithets as he strutted toward the former state policeman.

At that moment, the old trooper's broad fist shot between the bars and connected, dead center in the kidnapper's face. By the time Artie regained consciousness his wish had been granted. Coy had broken his nose with such force, that both eyes were swollen tightly shut. The only witness to the "accident" was Mark, who paused only long enough to take another bite of his apple and turn the page of the Marvel comic.

Three days before the New Year, Wells led a troupe that included Ted, Coy, and Carol toward an abandoned mine camp, eight miles southeast of Cunard. When Ted told of the Samaritan he'd met and wanted to repay somehow, it had suddenly become a new quest for Carol and the two old dynamos. After fighting old washed out roads and of course getting lost once or twice, Coy's Mercury drove right into the heart of beautiful downtown Hallelujah #1, the abandoned camp.

They were greeted by old' Leon, his wife Esther, and even Levon rolled his homemade wheelchair out to the door to see the commotion. Carol stood in awe, wide-eyed, staring at the black man.

"Dad!" Carol whispered.

"What ya' want Punkin?" he answered.

Then in a clear voice she asked, "Is his wife a coalminer too?"

"I don't think so."

"Then how'sa come they're so blacked up."

Leon chuckled audibly then stepped forward and dropped to one knee, "Honey, this is what color God made us. We're colored people."

"Is there more than you?"

"Oh yea, they'se bunches of us."

Carol stared inquisitively at the man kneeling before her then gently reached up and wiped her finger along his face. She nonchalantly glanced at her finger then frowned and nodded. She stepped a few feet back, placed her hand on her hips, and stared for a full half minute, then said, "Well by God, it looks good on ya."

Leon laughed for the better part of fifteen minutes.

New Years eve of the new 1953 found three men on the sun-porch of Wells' home, looking down at the small village below. It was cool here on the porch and with a sweater it was pleasant to be out. The old trooper and the coal baron sat opposite one another in noisy wicker. Snow was falling again and looked as though it may continue through the evening.

The young soldier chose to squat oriental style. He tapped a cigarette on his thumbnail as he peered warily over the banister through the glass.

This group had shared Christmas Eve and now they were ready to do the same for the New Year. Doreen still sported the bandage on her head. Carol would not be recovered from Christmas for several weeks. Everyone thought it best if she had a little extra special Christmas after her ordeal. Coy and Wells had taken to teasing Ted, in an effort to help him acclimate to regular society. Ted played along, awkwardly, trying desperately to fit back into a normal life.

"Hey boy," Coy started, "Why'd you go up ta' your room this evening after supper? You hafta take a nap or something?"

"Oh, it was something all right."

"She got ya' 'doing chores'?" Coy asked, in a semi-serious tone.

"Kinda," Ted answered, "her playin' catch up an' all."

"Sounds dangerous," taunted the trooper.

"'At's why I'm a hidin' out here," answered the soldier.

At that moment the front door opened and Carol walked out in her new pajamas, slippers, and housecoat. She walked up to Wells, smiled and asked, "Can I stay here with you and Coy for a while?"

Her dad stood out of the shadows, thinking she hadn't seen him. "Mom's lookin' for you again," she said with just a glance toward her father.

"Oh Lord," he muttered.

Just then, Helen stepped out on the porch, "Ted honey, could you help me with something in the house?" she asked sweetly.

"Oh, ok," Ted lowered his head and followed her. Just before he stepped through the door, Wells and Coy added their blessings.

"We'll be thinking about you, son."

"We'll say a prayer for ya', boy," Coy chuckled.

After he had gone, Wells said, "You know Coy, this town hasn't seen this much excitement in a hundred years."

"And it'll be another hundred," added the trooper.

The door opened and out stepped Doreen. "That bour..., I mean the coffee's ready in the kitchen, Coy. It's fixed the way you told me," she grinned. The trooper winked at the coal operator and gingerly followed the housekeeper with the turban bandages toward the kitchen for a dose of caffeine, and the bourbon, of course.

Carol curled up in the chair next to Wells, looked up and frowned. "Boy I hope my Dad gets better pretty soon," said Carol dryly.

"What makes you say that, Carol? He seems to be doing just fine to me," replied Wells.

"Well, Aunt Doreen says Mom is just 'a nurturing' Dad back to health…but, well, it's just hard ta' take sometimes."

"Oh? Why is it so hard to take Carol?"

"Well, I gotta act like I'm asleep when it starts on account o' it's kinda weird with my Mom actin' like that."

"It's probably best if you do just that," replied Wells.

"Well, she stares him down, and then she does like them wrestlers on the television does an' pins 'im down an' takes ta' bitin' 'im. Then they take their shirts off an' then he'll pin her for a while an' they'll wrestle for a while. Then she'll flip 'im back over an' hold 'em down till he gives an' all the while she's growlin' and gruntin', just like the wrestlers on the TV. I tell ya' it's just awful."

"I'm sure she's doing what she feels is best," Wells replied while suppressing his laughter.

"I s'pose she's doing it ta' get him tough agin, but it's not fun a' watching my daddy take a whuppin' like that all the time."

"I'll see what I can do about you getting a room of your own."

"Really?"

"Really. Happy New Year, Carol."

"Yea, I reckon." yawned the heathen.

Within a few short hours, the events of the preceding month were forgotten. It seems the man whose music swept the heartland of America to their feet with his foot-stompin' yodel as well as his haunting lonesome wail, came to the end of his trail that same morning there in Oak Hill. On New Years Day, Mr. Hank Williams gave up his ghost to the mountains of West Virginia.

THE END

AUTHOR'S NOTES

'Rag Doll Angel' is entirely fiction. The town of Oak Hill was used for historical purposes and this book reflects only a general resemblance of the town. I apologize to the people of Oak Hill for that confusion. I drew from the West Virginia towns of Bramwell and Shinnston but maintained the Oak Hill setting mostly because of the famous event at the 1953 New Year and because this region, with its chasms, mountains, whitewater, and the hardy saints who oversee this Eden, is one of the most beautiful areas in the United States. Thanks also to an unwitting rafting guide named 'Cat'.

My thanks also to my primary editor and sister Barbara M. Weaver for helping me gain control my rampant 'tale-spins'. To S.L. Gardner for her help in finalizing those spins. To my personal scribes, and sisters Jane and Twila. To an unending list of WVWriters, Inc. members, Morgantown Writers Group members, and 'The Crow's Quill' members for encouragement and support. To Tom, Mike, and Charlie for helping me to sort out cars, dates, trains, coal mine memories, and other nuances of that bygone era..

To my daughters, for unending inspiration.

To my parents, for never, ever trivializing the dreams of their children,

..........and my wife, for everything.

ABOUT THE AUTHOR

T.W. (Terry) McNemar is an award winning author and humorist. His work reflects the humanity, humor, and conscience of everyday life in the Appalachian Mountains that he calls home.

When asked about his style, he answered, “We all encounter various experiences, adventures, and events that we store – life might be a good word for it. That the information incubates or ferments is only as important as how it is played through our own minds eye. That is what gives individual writers their own voice. Mine has been an interesting journey, never boring, and I’m still headed upstream.”

His work has been featured in The Johns-Hopkins University ‘ScribblePress’, SUNY Press (Potsdam), Gerald R. Ratliff's *Young Women’s Monologues from Contemporary Plays*, MountainEchoes, an online literary journal, and Traditions, the literary journal of Fairmont State University.

`Terry and his family live near Clarksburg. He attended Fairmont State College (University) and is a graduate of Jim Comstock’s famous ‘University of Hard Knocks’ at Alderson-Broaddus College.

Printed in the United States
83612LV00003B/232-240/A

9 781601 452085